TINSEL TRICKERY

WINTER WITCHES OF HOLIDAY HAVEN BOOK 14

ELLE ADAMS

To be notified when Elle Adams's next book is released, sign up to her author newsletter.

The holiday season was upon us again, and this year's celebrations would be an occasion to remember.

Since it was always Christmas in Holiday Haven, hitting December wasn't necessarily a reason to celebrate any more than we usually did, but this year was set to be a special one. For one thing, the Holiday Haven Inn would be hosting an event to commemorate six years of introducing tourists to our particular brand of festive merriment. For another, my family was coming up to visit in time for the celebrations... and would also be meeting Spencer, my boyfriend of six months.

Hmm. Given last year's events, I might have to substitute the word "special" for "potentially catastrophic." My sister, Bella, had witnessed my tentative new relationship with Spencer get off the ground over the summer, but that wasn't the same as introducing my famously eccentric parents to him. After they'd gate-crashed the inn's five-year-anniversary celebrations last year, I'd been determined to avoid any unexpected surprises this time around, but I hadn't intended their meeting with Spencer to coincide with our biggest event of the year. Not to mention the annual Yule Ball, which was set to take place immediately afterwards.

That was the problem with having a boyfriend who worked for Holiday Haven's postal service during the busiest season of the year. It was a miracle Spencer had even been allowed to take Christmas itself off, and it'd taken a great deal of persuasion to convince his boss to let him attend our event as well as the Yule Ball. Hence my current dilemma. As I was in the middle of signing a group of guests out of the inn, my phone buzzed with yet another call from my parents' shared mobile phone back in England.

"Hey, Mum," I answered.

"Carol, which hats should we bring with us?" she asked.

I waved at the guests as they departed the inn through the front door. "I have no idea. Whichever you like."

"Red tinsel or green?" she pressed on. "I can't decide. Oh, and there's the reindeer hats… and the one shaped like a giant Christmas pudding…"

I stifled a groan. "Ask Dad. He's far more of an expert than I am."

"He's packing our cases. We have to fit in the turkey hat as well."

"Mum, please don't show up with a giant turkey on your head." She'd worn that hat once, and that had been more than enough to mentally scar me for life.

"Are you sure?" she asked. "I can bring the reindeer

one instead, then. Oh, and there's the one with the giant talking Santa head… which do I choose?"

"Pick the reindeer." That was the least offensive of the possible options. "It might upset Santa or Mrs Claus to hear about you wearing his head on top of your own."

"Oh, I meant for you, not me."

Okay, that was enough of that. "I don't need one. I have plenty of hats of my own." Normal-sized ones, that is. Unlike my parents, I liked being able to walk through doorways without showering everyone in glitter or getting my headwear stuck under the frame.

"You do?" she said. "Have you finally started using your magic?"

"I never stopped using it." *I just don't use my powers to make novelty hats.*

Admittedly, I'd spent most of my life reluctant to use the magical gifts that I'd inherited from my parents, but there were several good reasons for that, most of which involved experiencing deep-seated embarrassment every time my parents had ventured anywhere in public during the eighteen years I'd lived under their roof. Which was a lot. The way my parents' business was booming proved there was certainly a market for their magically crafted novelty hats, but I definitely wasn't among the target audience.

At least their excessive devotion to the festive season wouldn't be out of place in Holiday Haven… but that didn't mean their meeting with Spencer would go ahead without a hitch.

Behind Mum, I heard Dad shout in the background, "The suitcase won't close! I have to take out some of the hats!"

"Put them in the spare case!" Mum told him.

"This *is* the spare case," Dad replied.

"Er... how many cases are you packing, exactly?" I asked, not sure I wanted to know the answer.

"We narrowed it down to two each."

"How are you going to fly with those?" I had the sudden and unpleasant mental image of the two of them trying to steer broomsticks with their feet while their hands were occupied keeping hold of a stack of suitcases. "You know what, never mind."

When it came to my parents' dedication to their art, I'd learned not to ask too many questions. If they wanted to carry three dozen suitcases of novelty hats all the way up to the North Pole, there was very little I could do to stop them. It didn't hurt that they'd won a bunch of new fans here in Holiday Haven during their last visit, and that they'd sell most of the hats they brought to those fans during the intermission of our event.

"We'll manage," Mum told me. "I think your dad needs my help packing, but we'll talk again soon."

"Sure," I replied. "Have fun with the packing."

Mum ended the call while I put down my phone and resumed affixing the large welcome banner above the door to the inn's main hall. The words *Six Years of Festive Cheer* gleamed in green and red on the banner, and when I waved my hand, glitter streamed from my palm, and the letters started sparkling.

Behind the door, a faint thumping noise signalled that my best friend wasn't having much luck with decorating the hall.

"Are you sure the guests won't think we're recycling

the same props from last year's event?" I asked Mercy through the closed door.

A second muffled thud came from the other side. "Nope. Why fix what isn't broken?"

"True." I gave the banner a cursory examination and then added more sparkling glitter to the letters. The tree in the corner of the reception area was adorned in baubles marked with glittering number sixes, while clumps of holly with red berries hung above each doorframe. "Are you all right in there?"

"I'm fine." Another thud, followed by a curse. "Or not. Can you give me a hand with this?"

"Sure." I nudged open the door and ducked into the hall, which was full of stacked chairs ready to place in rows in front of the large stage at the front. Mercy was in the process of hanging up a long piece of tinsel at the top of a stepladder, but it'd come detached from the wall and now dangled sadly near the stage.

I crossed the hall, picked up the end of the tinsel, and stood on tiptoe to hand it to her. "I'm not tall enough for this. Wasn't Daryl available to help?"

"He's in rehearsals." She let out a stream of curses as the tinsel came detached from the wall the instant she let go of it.

"Hey, relax." I picked up the end of the tinsel again and passed it up to her. "We don't really need this many decorations in here, you know. The audience will be watching the stage, not the walls."

"I know." She blew out a breath. "I should have started the prep way in advance, though. I didn't count on Daryl getting invited to take part in that major Shakespearean production of *Twelfth Night* well as organising the play for our event. Not that I'm not happy for him… I'm glad he's going places."

"Me too." Daryl, her boyfriend, had been elected as the new leader of Holiday Haven's local theatre group and was therefore in charge of wrangling the other performers in line for the festive-themed play that would form part of our event. We'd got a star-studded cast on board—well, as star-studded as was possible in Holiday Haven, anyway—and now we were on the final push to pull everything together.

Mercy fixed up the end of the tinsel again, which stayed put this time, hanging in loops from the wall. She climbed down the ladder and gave a heavy sigh that seemed directed at the hall in general.

"What's up?" I asked her. "You weren't this stressed last year."

"We set a new standard then," she said. "We have to do the same as the last show, only better."

"Last time was nearly a disaster," I reminded her. "We had to pull together at the last second. This time we have more lead time, and it doesn't hurt that I know my parents will be here, hats and all.. We won't be blindsided like before."

To my eternal surprise, their hats had been a major hit with the attendees, so much so that they'd even set up an order form for this year's event so attendees could collect their purchased hats in person. I didn't understand in the slightest, but then again, I'd grown up surrounded by hat-related nonsense. The fact that we were now advertising the "novelty hat sale" on our posters and flyers for the event proved I'd got past some of my reluctance, but I drew the line at using my magical skills to make any hats myself.

"Yeah…" Mercy trailed off. "You're right, though. I'm starting to think I should have picked another theme for the event instead of doing the same as last year."

"No, it's fine," I said hastily. "I didn't mean to add to your stress by making that suggestion. I'm sure there are plenty of people who weren't here last year who are looking forward to the experience, and the others won't mind it being the same. They never get tired of the carollers, do they?"

While sometimes it was nice to have a change from the usual, this was the time of year when everything festive and seasonal came out in full force, so we'd decked the halls with every bough of holly we could find. Everything was prepared, despite the tight schedule, and my parents' rooms were ready for their arrival. We didn't need to mix things up when they worked just fine as they were.

"I guess not," Mercy said. "Ah… what does Gerry want this time?"

Through the partly open door, I saw our only current guest, Gerry, walk into the reception area. "I'll find out."

I left the hall and ducked back behind the desk to face our visitor. Gerry always wore a suit and tie under a garment that resembled a dressing gown crossed with a cape. He claimed to be a stage magician in training and had recently adopted the stage name "Geronimo."

"Hello." He gave me his usual vague smile. "Can I order a martini?"

At eleven in the morning? "We don't usually do room service, but I'll tell Kaitlyn to take you one. It shouldn't be a problem."

"Okay." His brow furrowed. "Oh, that's right… it's Janice who offers room service at her inn. I tried to get a room there, but she didn't have any space this week."

My mouth parted. "Like I said, Kaitlyn will bring it to your room."

I watched him leave, wondering if he'd intended to insult me or not. If it was anyone other than Gerry speaking, I'd have been certain that mentioning Janice's inn had been an intentional jab, but Gerry was likely as oblivious to the implications of his words as he was to pretty much everything else. Kaitlyn, the elf who did most of the cleaning at the inn, was used to carrying out the guests' strange demands, so I passed on his request to her while she cleaned the tables in the inn's restaurant.

When Gerry had first shown up, I'd wondered if he'd shown up hoping to take part in the event, but it'd taken him three days to even notice we were preparing to host a celebration. At least I wasn't too worried about how he'd react to my parents' arrival in a few days, given his own eccentricities. Certain other guests of ours had been more problematic, like the ones we'd hosted back in the summer. Having the Easter Bunny, Cupid, the Tooth Fairy, and the Fairy Godmother at the inn at the same time made our current schedule seem tame, though since that debacle had ended in my first date with Spencer, I couldn't really complain.

Mercy's voice drifted over from the hall. "Was that Gerry?"

"Yeah, he wanted a martini." I kept my voice low. "He mentioned Janice does room service. He hasn't stayed at *her* inn before, has he?"

A thud and a curse sounded in response. Grimacing, I

opened the door to see that the tinsel had fallen off the wall entirely, lying curled on the floor like a long silvery snake.

Mercy slumped down against the stage. "I give up. We need to find another decoration."

"Wrap the tinsel around the base of the stage instead," I suggested. "That way it can't fall down. I'll come up with something for the walls, no problem."

"Thanks, Carol," said Mercy. "I didn't realise how lucky I had it when everyone chose to do their rehearsals here last year instead of at the studio."

"Lucky?" I raised a brow. "Have you forgotten the part where the entire theatre group accidentally got turned into frogs?"

She gave a wry smile. "I guess. What can we try instead?"

"Something smaller," I decided. "Or my parents will donate some spare hats to hang on the walls instead. It sounds like they're bringing all their stock."

"Wow, business must be going well," she remarked. "They want to sell them at reception before and after the show, right?"

"That's the plan," I confirmed. "Mercy, it's going to be fine. We have more time to get the inn ready if we don't have people walking in and out and leaving bits of their costumes everywhere. They won't have to deal with my parents either."

"Unless they show up early."

"They might, but I'm asking them to forewarn me." I'd made it clear that I'd appreciate more than an hour's notice after they'd shown up on our doorstep last year unexpectedly and thrown our plans into disarray. "They keep calling me every few hours to ask questions about hats, so I'm sure they'll tell me if there's a change in plans."

"I think it'd be strange if they *weren't* calling to ask about hats," she said. "What did Gerry say about Janice, anyway?"

"He told me she offered room service for her guests. That's new."

Janice ran the inn nearest to ours and had been our rival for the duration of our time in Holiday Haven, though our mutual animosity had abated over the past year.

"Even she gets an original idea once in a while." Mercy pulled a face. "I don't want to see what *she* comes up with for her Christmas celebration this year."

"You mean what she borrows from us." Given her habit of mimicking our own strategies, I expected her to come up with an event that echoed our own. If anything, I'd be disappointed if she didn't, and it wasn't as if she could bring my parents along to sell hats at her own event, after all. "She can't hold a candle to us, Mercy. Don't give it any thought."

This role reversal surprised me a little. Of the two of us, I was usually the one who tended to overthink the potential disasters from any given situation—mostly because disaster had followed wherever my family had set foot for my entire life, and even moving here to Holiday Haven hadn't entirely quelled my instinct to prepare for the worst.

It wasn't until recently that I'd begun to appreciate that my parents had given me an infinitely more interesting life than I otherwise would have experienced, and I'd absorbed more of their values than I'd thought. I mean, my plan to escape them had involved flying to the North Pole and opening an inn, which wasn't the sort of idea that'd occur to the average person.

As I returned to the reception area, a small, fluffy owl bobbed into view, little wings beating, and dropped a small box on the counter.

"Oh, good, our latest order's here," I called to Mercy.

"Sounds like yours is too."

"Ha ha."

Sunbeam was Spencer's assistant and a post owl in training. Due to the owl's small size, he was only able to carry the smallest packages, but he did so with great enthusiasm. His mentor, as Mercy had rightly guessed, wasn't far behind him. As I beckoned Sunbeam to land on my shoulder, Spencer walked in through the front door, his face flushed from the cold and his dark hair curling into his eyes. He shot me a grin from under a fur hat—normal sized, thankfully—and beckoned Sunbeam to return to his hand.

"Hey." He greeted me with a hug and kiss. "What did you order this time?"

"Haven't a clue. Mercy bought something for our event, I assume."

"I thought it might be more craft supplies."

"Nah, we have enough of those." Though delivering packages to the inn gave Spencer an excuse to spend time with me that he wouldn't normally have had. "I can order another one if it means I get a visit tomorrow as well."

"Yeah…" He didn't quite return my smile, his brow crinkling as if frustrated.

"What is it?" I asked. "Is that co-worker of yours being a nuisance again?"

"Maybe," he answered cryptically. "It might be nothing, but one of the packages I delivered this morning seems to have gone missing. I swear I left it outside the right house, but when the customer called our office, they were pretty adamant that it was never there."

"You mean… someone stole it?"

"That's what I thought," he said. "Until a second parcel I delivered vanished from a totally different customer's address. Needless to say, Dennis isn't thrilled with me."

Oh, boy. The boss—who his employees called "Dennis the Menace" behind his back—was not exactly the forgiving type. "That's hardly your fault."

Whether another employee was responsible or not, the thief had picked the worst time possible to strike. Who'd steal packages right before Christmas?

2

"Is there anything I can do to help find the missing packages?" I asked Spencer.

"I know you're busy, and I don't want to add to your problems," he said. "I just wanted to give you a warning in case I'm not sent to deliver packages to you for a while. Dennis will see to that."

"You can't be blamed for something you had nothing to do with," I protested. "If someone is stealing packages from under your boss's nose, then it's a legitimate problem. Especially if they're specifically targeting packages you delivered."

"Two packages might be a coincidence," he told me. "I just find it weird that both customers claimed their packages were never delivered at all. If the owner isn't in, I always make sure I put the parcels in a place they can't be seen by anyone else."

"I'm sure you do, and I bet your boss knows it too," I reassured him. "It might be a mistake on the part of the customers. Or a particularly sneaky thief."

ELLE ADAMS

"Might be." He blew out a breath. "I shouldn't come here to complain to you, though. I know you have your hands full."

"I have a bit of free time now," I said. "We only have one guest at the moment, at least until my parents get here."

"Until..." He trailed off. "I forgot. When is that?"

"Friday, and don't worry, I've warned them not to bombard you with too many questions."

"I'm sure they aren't *that* bad," he said. "I've been dealing with customers for years, remember? Being accused of stealing my own packages is far from the strangest issue I've had to deal with."

"Trust me, my parents make the carollers look morose," I warned. "They fit right in here, but a first-time meeting is best faced with a stiff drink."

He grinned. "I'll keep that in mind. I did have *some* idea of what I was getting into when we started dating, remember?"

"Definitely." I couldn't forget easily, given that he'd come into my life right in the middle of the madness at the summer solstice and we'd somehow put together a relationship in the ensuing chaos. What was a little parental mayhem compared to that? "My parents aren't the important thing right now, though. We need to find your missing packages. Where do you want to start? The post office?"

"Sure," he said. "I really appreciate this, you know. I'll have to come up with a way to repay you."

"Getting to spend more time with you is reward enough."

The door inched open behind me, and I turned to find

Mercy peering out of the back room.

"Is it okay if I run out to help Spencer with an errand? I'll set up the decorations as soon as I get back."

"You two are going out?"

"Yeah, there's been some kind of mix-up at the post office," I said. "Possibly someone stealing packages. I offered to help so Spencer's boss doesn't come down too hard on him."

"Sure, go ahead." She closed the door behind her and admired the banner I'd put up. "I'll watch the desk. It'll be a nice break from decorating."

"Cheers."

I left the inn with Spencer, Sunbeam flitting alongside us. It began to snow as we walked, and I had to rescue the little owl from being swept away in a swirl of snowflakes a couple of times.

"Is he always going to be this tiny?" I asked Spencer the second time this happened.

"I think he is," he said. "Which means he's going to have to stick to delivering small packages, unless a bigger owl offers to help him. Some of them find him annoying, but the owl postmaster doesn't seem to mind him."

"Good. What about your supervisor?"

He shook his head. "That's a whole other issue. Dennis is adamant that he'll never be a real post owl, but now I've gone and distracted him with this package fiasco. The thing is, Travis was the last person who delivered a parcel to the same area I went to. I can see him sneaking in and stealing one of my packages to mess with me, but doing the same to another parcel right afterwards is excessive."

No kidding. Why Travis, his co-worker, would try to

sabotage someone as mild-mannered as Spencer was a mystery to me.

"Why would he want to mess with your deliveries in the first place?" I asked.

"Because he's annoyed with me," he replied. "He's always slacking off, so I called him out on it, which landed me on his bad side."

"I understand the type, believe me."

"I've been expecting him to retaliate for a while, but he's been sneakier than I expected," he said. "He'll deny having anything to do with the missing parcels without proof."

Annoying co-workers were one of the reasons Mercy and I had set up our business together and only hired people who didn't make us want to tear out our hair. Janice had been an annoyance for a while, but at least we'd never had to work inside the same building as her, and Spencer's experience was a reminder that Holiday Haven had given us an opportunity that many people didn't have. We'd been lucky.

When we reached the post office, Spencer peered in through the window before leading me into the building and through a door to a large room where the human staff worked under the watchful eyes of their owl supervisors.

Several people seated at long tables glanced up in curiosity when they saw us but quickly returned to their work. No surprise there, because the tables were piled high with towering stacks of letters and teetering heaps of parcels. The sheer amount of mail that passed through Holiday Haven at this time of year meant all the postal staff were constantly rushed off their feet, so anyone who wanted to intentionally make trouble would get zero leniency from their supervisor. If they got caught, that is.

"Travis isn't here," Spencer whispered in my ear. "Still out doing deliveries, I assume. I don't see my supervisor anywhere, so we can have a look around, but try not to knock anything over."

"You don't think the packages are hidden in the office, do you?"

"If Travis took them, I don't think he'd have been stupid enough to hide them in here," he murmured. "But it's worth a look around to see if he got careless and left a clue behind him."

"True." Though there was a slight issue with his idea. Pretty much every surface in the room was covered in parcels, letters, and envelopes, and finding a single package in here was as likely as a heatwave at the North Pole. "You might want to give me an idea of what the packages actually look like. It's kind of a needle-in-a-haystack situation here. Or a strand of hay in a haystack, rather."

"The first parcel contained a bicycle," Spencer said. "I think that's pretty noticeable."

"Yeah... that would stand out," I acknowledged. "And the second?"

"A carved reindeer rocking horse. Solid mahogany."

"How'd someone sneak off with that?" They'd need the cooperation of a few post owls. Or a sledge. In any case, both packages were too bulky to be hidden inside a drawer or cabinet, or even underneath the desks. The only possible place was one of the offices at the back which belonged to the bosses, but Spencer dismissed that idea.

"The thief wouldn't have access to the supervisors' offices," he explained. "Dennis, for one, would definitely notice an unexpected package under his desk. We'll look outside instead."

I followed him out of the office, relieved that the snow seemed to be slowing down. While I generally appreciated the wintry weather, trekking all over town in a blizzard in search of the missing packages didn't appeal. "You think he hid them out in the snow?"

"I don't see him making the effort to haul them back to the office," he replied. "No, there's a stronger chance they might be hidden near the actual houses they were meant to be delivered to. They can't have vanished into thin air."

"You have the addresses?"

"I do," he said. "Are you sure you want to come along? It's quite a walk."

"Of course I am," I insisted. "This is the first time I've been able to get outside in a while. I could use the fresh air."

The air was certainly fresh, and it was a good job I didn't mind the cold, given that the only time Holiday Haven had deviated from its usual snowy weather was during the summer solstice event six months ago when a sunny bubble had been confined to a small area of town. Otherwise, it was a white Christmas every day of the year, which suited me just fine. Snowmen sat on the corners, groups of carollers regaled anyone who walked past, and everything was aglow with the cheer of the holiday season.

The first victim of the mysterious package thief lived in a sizeable house that sat behind a wooden fence. Sunbeam amused himself by chasing snowflakes around while Spencer and I scanned the area outside the house for any hidden packages.

"Whereabouts did you leave it?" I asked Spencer.

He indicated the area next to the front porch, where a cluster of holly bushes grew beside the front door. "It took a lot of finesse to hide it in there without waking up the—"

A growl interrupted his words, followed by the thump of several sets of footsteps. Or rather, paws. A pair of giant hounds came sprinting up to the fence, jaws slavering, eyes fixated on Spencer and me.

"Ah." I took a step back. "Security guards?"

Spencer stepped back alongside me. "Yes, and the reason I had to replace my last pair of boots."

One of the hounds slammed into the gate, and it screamed against its hinges. When the second hound joined it, Spencer and I backed away and then legged it down the street. Sunbeam zipped overhead in a frantic bundle of feathers, while the sound of growls and snarls pursued us. It wasn't until we'd rounded several corners that the beasts finally gave up the chase, letting us recover and catch our breaths.

"Sorry." Spencer caught Sunbeam in his palm, giving the owl a reassuring stroke with his other hand. "I didn't know they'd be that on edge."

"How did anyone steal a package from underneath their noses?" I gasped, bent double against a stitch in my chest. "You'd think the thief would have run away the instant those creatures showed up."

"I have no idea," he said. "Trust me, I'm just as confused as you are. Maybe the dogs were napping earlier and are now trying to make up for lost time, but we can't exactly ask them for their perspective."

"Pity they don't have security cameras on the property," I remarked.

"I thought the same." Spencer released Sunbeam, who returned to chasing snowflakes around. "As it happens, the second victim of the thief's work *might* have security cameras. He's certainly rich enough to, but I didn't ask when I delivered the package."

"Rich people often have them," I agreed. "Is it worth a look?"

"Might be," he said. "Mr Carlisle doesn't have any security dogs, but he does have a gate fitted with an intercom to talk to his security. I had to talk my way through to get in to deliver the package in the first place."

"Wait, doesn't that mean his security will remember you were there?" I asked.

"No, they let me in without meeting me face-to-face," he replied. "That apparently wasn't enough for Mr Carlisle, who told the office I never delivered the package at all."

"That makes zero sense." Regardless, I followed him down the street until we reached a large manor house surrounded by high fences. "Whoa. Is this the place?"

Spencer nodded while I admired the sheer size of the property. Snow covered the wide roofs and the tops of the arched windows, while the grounds were vast enough to fit a whole sledge track in. And a pack of dogs.

"Nothing's going to attack us, are they?" I asked warily.

"No." He approached the wide gates at the front and hit a button that rang a loud buzzer.

A voice came from behind the gate. "Give me the password."

"The password is 'Rudolph,'" Spencer said clearly. "I'm here with the delivery Mr Carlisle ordered."

Another buzz followed, then there was a crackling sound.

"You have to give a password to get in?" I studied the gates, which remained closed and unyielding.

"Mr Carlisle leaves the day's password with the post office when he makes the order," he explained to me. "If you get the password wrong, then you have to stand outside and hope an actual person comes to let you in. Not much fun in a blizzard."

"Ouch."

How had the thief circumvented that? They might have eavesdropped on Spencer and learned the password that way, but it didn't seem worth the hassle for the sake of a practical joke. Especially on top of the package being made of solid mahogany. Yet I was out of any other possible explanations for where it had vanished to.

The gate creaked inward, allowing us into the grounds. I took a wary step across the threshold of the gate while Spencer took the lead—then halted.

A middle-aged man wearing bright-red snow boots walked towards us, and he looked at us with an expression of marked disdain. "And you are?"

"Mr Carlisle," said Spencer. "I'm the person who delivered your package earlier. I know it was reported missing, but I came through your gates and brought it to the house myself."

"Really," Mr Carlisle said flatly. "I came outside to pick

up the package and found nothing there. Unless this is your idea of a joke?"

"Certainly not," said Spencer. "I take my job seriously, especially at this time of year, and I want to help find your missing parcel."

Mr Carlisle looked disbelieving, but at least we had yet to be attacked by any more security dogs.

"Do you have security cameras?" I asked him.

"No," he replied. "I don't trust them not to spy on my family."

I blinked. "Erm... what about recordings of the people who gave the password to get in?"

"I don't allow any kind of recording equipment on my property."

"Then who listens to the passwords?" asked Spencer. "Someone opened the gate."

"I listen to them myself."

This just got weirder and weirder. "Then you know Spencer was here. You heard his voice earlier, right?"

"That doesn't mean he brought what he was hired to," said Mr Carlisle. "Now if you don't mind, I need to purchase an alternative present for my son since the last one *vanished*. Who are you, anyway? You're not one of the post office staff."

"I'm helping Spencer." This was going well. "Can we have a look around the grounds? Maybe it... er, got buried in snow somewhere."

My nerve faltered when Mr Carlisle glowered at me. "No, you may not enter my property. As for you, *delivery boy*, I'm severely disappointed in the postal service. If you ruin the holidays for my entire family, then I'll be sure to let everyone in town know of your shoddy work."

"We're working hard to make sure your delivery is returned to you," said Spencer.

"I'll believe that when I see it." Mr Carlisle turned his back. "The package I ordered is nowhere on my property."

From what I could see of the snowy grounds behind him, he was right. I didn't think it was possible for someone to have just misplaced a giant carved rocking horse, even in a house this size, especially when it required more than one person to actually lift the package. Mr Carlisle clearly wasn't budging, so we retreated from the grounds with our tails between our legs. Except Sunbeam, who happily bounced along until Spencer shushed him firmly.

"Weird," I commented. "I'd have thought he'd have cameras around."

"That's what I thought," he said. "Guess not, though. Perhaps I should have sent someone else to search the place, but nobody was free."

"Why not go back to the post office and ask?" I suggested. "In fact, where is that Travis guy?"

"I haven't the faintest idea, and I doubt he'd admit to anything without proof." He scowled over his shoulder at the house. "I don't know *how* he got through security, if it was him. I don't see Mr Carlisle buying his excuses, if they're anything like the reasons he comes up with for slacking off."

"Does he have magical abilities?" I asked, unable to think of any other way anyone could have got the package off Mr Carlisle's property without being detected.

"No," he said. "None whatsoever. And I don't think he knows anyone else who'd be willing to use magic to screw with me, but I might be wrong on that one."

A buzzing noise startled me before I realised it was coming from Spencer's pocket. "Someone's calling you."

Spencer fished out his phone. "Nah, it's my supervisor messaging me... That's weird."

"What?"

He frowned. "Dennis got a call from someone on the other side of town who unexpectedly received a bike as a delivery instead of what he ordered. Specifically, the bike that was supposed to be at the house of the owner of those two guard dogs."

"The other side of town?" I echoed. "How'd it get there?"

"I don't know," he said, "but what are the odds of the same happening to the rocking horse?"

"I'd say there's a fair chance."

"Yeah." Spencer glanced behind him at the closed gates to Mr Carlisle's property. "At least they were delivered *somewhere,* but what would be the point?"

"No clue," I said. "At least they can't blame you for moving the packages. There's no way you could have done it."

I hoped they wouldn't, but it was clear that something far stranger than simple thievery was going on here.

3

Spencer and I parted ways at the post office—him to fetch the package and redeliver it to its intended recipient, and me to return to the inn. I'd told him that I didn't mind going with him, but he insisted that I didn't need to trail back and forth from one end of town to the other twice in a single day. I'd made him promise to text me if the second package ever showed up and then left to go and help Mercy instead.

Upon reaching the inn, I kicked the last of the snow off my boots before leaving them near the door.

Mercy waved at me from behind the front desk. "Find your thief?"

"Nope, but we found something weirder."

I gave her a rundown of the past hour or so, starting with the missing packages and ending with our discovery that our dedicated thief had seemingly swapped the packages with others on complete opposite ends of town.

"That's dedication," said Mercy. "Do you think the other package will turn up too?"

"I'd say the odds are decently high, but I'm lost on how they managed to move something that size around without drawing attention."

"Not to mention get past the security," she added. "I can't believe that guy requires a password to get onto his property but doesn't believe in cameras."

"Tell me about it," I said. "As for the other guy, I hope he's called off his security dogs so Spencer can actually take him his delivery."

Though between being chased by security hounds and getting into trouble with his boss, Spencer didn't have much of a choice. At least the customer ought to have their delivery in time for the holidays without any more deviations, or at least without any that could be blamed on Spencer. As for the other package... I was willing to bet it'd show up in similar circumstances.

"Who moved the packages, do you know?" asked Mercy.

"Spencer told me there's this co-worker of his who doesn't like him, but as far as pranks go, this is a bit of an extreme one."

"No kidding," she said. "Does this co-worker have any magical talents?"

"None, according to Spencer," I said. "I guess he might have asked someone else to help him out, but it doesn't seem likely. Anyway, the delivery had better stay where it's put this time."

"Yeah," said Mercy. "It's been pretty quiet here. Gerry came in asking for another margarita, but it turned out he lost the first one."

I frowned. "How'd he lose it?"

"He put it on the windowsill to cool down."

"Right…" With Gerry, it probably wasn't worth pressing for the details.

"I'm glad he's our only guest," she added. "This is hard enough to handle without adding demanding guests on top of it."

"Like my parents?"

"They aren't demanding," she reassured me. "Besides, we have a few days till they show up."

"It'll take them that long to pack their suitcases."

"You aren't wrong," she said. "At least they're easily entertained, because I think we'll be tweaking the event schedule until the last minute. Half the theatre group has come down with flu."

"Oh, no." A pause. "Not Daryl?"

"Nope, but he's having to pick up the slack for the others." She rested her elbows on the desk. "As usual."

"Sounds like Spencer," I remarked with sympathy. "He's having to run around doing extra deliveries because certain co-workers of his keep slacking off."

"I'm hoping we can turn this around," said Mercy. "Daryl's reassigning roles to new cast members. It's a good job all the cast learn each other's lines, because they'd be in trouble if they didn't."

"Good job," I agreed. "It wouldn't be a Holiday Haven Inn event without a few unexpected surprises, would it?"

"I guess not."

Seeing the event come together in the end would be worth it. Once we caught the mysterious package thief, anyway.

———

I didn't hear from Spencer again until the following morning. My phone began to buzz with an incoming call while Mercy and I were finishing up breakfast.

"Hey, Spencer," I answered, taking my phone out of the restaurant and into the lobby. "Anything new?"

"I have good news and bad news," said Spencer. "The good news is that the second package showed up."

"Where?" I asked.

"At the North Pole. I had to take a sledge there to fetch it back."

"And that's the *good* news? What's the bad?"

"The bad news is that the exact same thing happened again today with a different package, and the intended recipient is not thrilled, since it was a present for her fiancé and she wanted it to be delivered in time for the holidays."

"Again?" So much for this being a one-time prank. "Ah —have you seen Travis today at all?"

"Yes, and he seems to find the situation hilarious."

I arched a brow. "Any concrete proof that he did it?"

"No, and I'm trying to figure out how it was even possible," he said. "If he's the mastermind, he'd need outside help."

"An accomplice," I surmised. "That does sound like a lot of trouble to go to for a simple prank, but if he's that petty, then you never know."

"Exactly," he said. "I'm not sure how to catch him in the act, though. If he's specifically targeting my deliveries, then he's probably doing it while I'm out of the office and I'm not able to watch him."

"Hmm." I thought. "If you deliver the next package to the intended address and then wait outside and watch from a distance, then you might see his spell in the act."

"You mean I might see the package disappear?" he said. "I might, but there'd be no way for me to tell whereabouts it actually disappeared to."

"True." I glanced behind me at Mercy, who'd left the restaurant ahead of Gerry. "All right. If you have someone watching Travis while you're delivering the package, then we might be able to catch him in the act."

"Who can I drag away from their job at a time like this?" From his tone, he was shaking his head in frustration. "It's not fair of me to risk getting another person into trouble like that."

"Did you not hear me say 'we'?" I'd already finished making the new decorations for the hall the previous night, and it wouldn't take me long to put them up. Since my parents wouldn't be arriving for another two days, I had a bit of time to kill. "I'll meet you at the post office?"

"You don't have to—"

"It's no bother. I'll just check with Mercy."

Mercy was already nodding, guessing what I planned to do. "Go ahead."

"Mercy says it's fine," I told Spencer. "I'll meet you at work."

I hung up on his protests and went to get my coat and boots. While Spencer's co-workers might have been willing to help out, Spencer needed someone on his team who wasn't preoccupied trying to deliver gifts to hundreds of people in the space of a few days. Besides, if someone wanted to get my boyfriend into trouble, then I'd see to it that they didn't get away with it. If I'd inherited one trait from my parents, it was the inherent stubbornness needed to keep a business running against all the odds.

Besides, Spencer had come through for me countless times when I needed his help at the inn. The guy was a handy mechanic and skilled at DIY, where I had no talent in that area. My own magical skills wouldn't be much help in this scenario, but whoever was behind this prank doubtless didn't expect Spencer to have brought backup to spy on the post office.

As planned, Spencer was waiting for me outside the post office, his eyes shadowed with tiredness and his face flushed with the cold.

"I owe you one," he said when he saw me. "Really."

I hugged him. "I told you, I have nothing happening today except fielding calls from my parents about which hats to bring."

His mouth curved in a grin. "Meanwhile, I have an endless list of deliveries on my schedule, at least two of which are currently *not* where they're supposed to be. Also, Travis is in the office, so either he sent someone else to mess with my deliveries or he's learned to teleport."

"He's been inside the office the whole time you were out?"

"Today, certainly," he said. "That's why I'm not keen on making an outright accusation. If you can watch him from outside, I'll head off to my next delivery and text you when I'm there."

"I'll see if he leaves the office," I agreed. "Sure, I can do that. Though he might notice me spying on him."

"I thought that, so I came up with a plan." He indicated the path alongside the building. "This way."

Intrigued, I followed him around the corner, where

several snowy trees flanked the building on its left-hand side. The window at the side showed the post room and the staff sorting packages and envelopes within, handing them to owls to ferry outside.

"You can see pretty much everything from this angle," Spencer told me. "Including Travis."

"True, but they can see me too."

"Nobody in there is looking out the window. They're far too busy with the packages… and our target isn't even facing this way." He indicated a man sitting with his back to the window. "That's him. Travis."

I couldn't make out much of his appearance except pale skin and dark hair shaved in a buzz cut. The man's movements were sullen as he tossed envelopes from one pile into another, and he didn't look up.

"Like I said, he finds the package situation hilarious," Spencer said in a low voice. "He's also likely to be slacking off, but he won't expect anyone to be watching him from behind. He pretends to be productive whenever the supervisor is around."

"Is Dennis watching, then?" I instinctively ducked my head.

"Yes, and I'm likely to get into trouble if he finds me lurking around outside instead of delivering my packages. Just keep your head down, and you'll be fine."

"All right," I said. "I'll let you know if I see Travis doing anything suspicious."

Wait. What counted as suspicious in a room full of magical gifts and talking delivery owls?

"If he's working with someone else, he'll be messaging them or otherwise communicating," he murmured. "Or else they'll be hiding in the area too."

"So I might run into them."

"Exactly," he replied. "If you want to take the risk, then keep Sunbeam with you to keep an eye out for trouble."

I raised a brow. "Can Sunbeam be quiet and calm for long enough to spy on someone?"

"Fair point," he said. "Everyone's used to him bouncing around, though, and if you keep him out here and someone happens to glance out the window, then he's likely to distract them from seeing you. I'll fetch him."

He trekked back towards the building and whistled a faint tune. The little owl appeared a moment later and zipped over to my side.

"Ready to help Carol out?" Spencer asked.

The owl let out a hoot of excited agreement, which caused several people to look up inside the office. I hastily ducked my head again, while Spencer gave the owl a few whispered instructions.

"I hope you're okay with this," Spencer added to me. "Let me know if you need me to come back, and I'll be right here."

"I did say I'd be fine, right?" I squeezed his arm. "Let me help you for a change."

"Yes, but I'm asking you to... not exactly break the law, but to act a little ethically dubiously."

"Travis is the one being ethically dubious if he's trying to sabotage your deliveries," I pointed out. "Not to mention he's making things unfair for all the people who want mail to be delivered on time for the holidays too."

"True." He gave me a brief hug and kiss. "Text me if you need me."

"Good luck." I waved him off and then caught Sunbeam in the palm of my hand before he could follow him. "You're staying with me. Think you can keep still so we can catch Travis in the act?"

Sunbeam's head bobbed in agreement.

For a while, I amused myself by teaching Sunbeam to follow commands, some of which he excelled at and others not so much. At least it kept us both entertained while we waited for Travis to do something that attracted our attention. He didn't seem to notice he was being watched while simply tossing packages and envelopes into careless heaps. I hoped he was paying some attention, considering they were probably someone's Christmas cards, but I had my doubts.

After an hour or so, my phone pinged with a message from Spencer. *Delivered the package. Let's see what happens.*

I peered at Travis through the window from my vantage point between the trees. He'd stopped sorting packages, and his head was bent over his mobile phone, but I couldn't see if he was messaging someone or just screwing around on the internet when he thought nobody was paying attention. I'd need to be standing directly behind him in order to see his screen, so I crept closer and peered through the glass. He'd angled the phone so that the desk concealed it from sight, and even being against the window wasn't close enough for me to confirm if he was messaging someone or not.

I darted behind the tree again and whispered to Sunbeam, "Can you get behind Travis and see what he's doing on his phone?"

Sunbeam nodded eagerly before flying over to the window and perching on the edge. His little wings beat as he flew higher and perched on the rim of the upper part of the window. The glass shifted a little. I hadn't realised the window was open the faintest crack, but when Sunbeam perched on the edge, the gap widened.

"Sunbeam," I hissed. "No. Get back here."

He didn't pay me any attention. Instead, he hopped on the edge until the top part of the window swung wide open, sending him tumbling head over heels into the office.

Right on top of Travis.

I choked on a laugh at Travis's expression of shock at being hit by what resembled a fluffy tennis ball, but he dislodged the owl and spun around on the spot, his gaze landing on my hiding spot. Uh-oh.

There was no point in pretending I hadn't been there, so I gave him a sheepish look and mouthed *sorry*.

He narrowed his eyes and turned away, roughly picking up the owl in one hand before walking out of sight. My heart gave an unpleasant lurch, but the idea of running off and abandoning Sunbeam didn't appeal. Besides, if nothing else, I might get to have a chat with Spencer's notorious rival and see if he gave anything away.

I waited at the side of the building until Travis came stomping outside with the little owl clutched in his palm.

"Is this yours?" he growled, holding out Sunbeam.

"Sorry about him." I reached out a hand, and Sunbeam happily hopped onto my palm. "He got a bit overexcited about coming to work."

"What are you doing out here?" He indicated the trees. "You don't work here."

"I'm waiting for Spencer," I lied. "I brought Sunbeam to help him. He accidentally left him at the inn."

Sunbeam bounced up and down and nodded his little head in agreement.

Travis didn't look convinced. "Do you normally hide in the bushes to wait for him?"

"No, but I didn't want anyone to think I was loitering." Which was… exactly what I was doing. "I thought the supervisor might be annoyed to find me outside."

His disbelieving expression faded a little. "Yeah, he would, but it's Spencer's own fault for being careless."

"Really?" I feigned surprise. "Don't you two get along?"

He snorted. "No. The guy thinks he's in charge. He's obnoxious."

Hmm. His tone conveyed annoyance, but not maliciousness. Not enough for me to have a definitive answer on whether he was behind the parcel incidents or not.

"Do you know when he'll be back?" I asked casually. "I heard there was some kind of mix-up with the packages earlier, so I think he's sorting that out."

Amusement flickered into his expression. "Serves him right for being an overachiever."

"You mean doing his job?" I studied his face. "Do you have the same problem with any of your other co-workers?"

"No, but none of them talk to me like I'm five." He scowled. "It's annoying."

"Does anyone else feel that way?"

He gave me a curious look. "I don't know. Why do you care?"

"Because I'm dating him." That, at least, wasn't a lie. "Believe it or not, I actually want to see him this Christmas, and I can't do that if he's being rushed off his feet trying to do other people's work."

His eyes narrowed a fraction. "Don't give me that look. I didn't do a thing to his deliveries. I hardly want Dennis to get any more agitated than he already is."

Hmm. If not him, then who had done it? It didn't sound like he liked Dennis any more than Spencer did, but that didn't mean he hadn't intended to land Spencer in trouble with the boss.

I shrugged. "I mean, it's not great timing, with the holidays and everything."

"It's always the holidays" was his reply.

"Yes, but you know what I mean. The post office is busier at this time of year than any other."

"Only because we don't have enough staff."

Or because certain people are slacking off. "Have you mentioned that to your boss?"

"No. I don't want to work on Christmas Day myself, you know." He scoffed, eyeing Sunbeam. "As for the post owls, Spencer is wasting his time with that one."

Sunbeam gave an indignant hoot.

"I don't think so." I gave the little owl a reassuring stroke on his fluffy head. "Don't you have work to do?"

"You're as bad as he is." He made a derisive noise. "Did he put you up to this?"

"No, of course not." I shook my head. "You aren't *that* important to him, you know."

I'd probably pay the price for my rudeness, but he was the one who'd insulted Sunbeam, and if Travis was behind the pranks, then I'd have all the more reason to catch him in the act.

Travis went back into the office without looking back, while Sunbeam shuffled his feathers in annoyance. When the door closed, I whispered, "Ignore him. Also, maybe next time you should check the window is open before jumping on it."

I was the one who'd sent him to the window in the first place, though, and I'd little expected to have an actual conversation with Travis as a result. I'd learned a handful of things, such as that Travis's attitude towards his job had much to be desired.

But did that necessarily translate to guilt, or was I reading too much into it because both Spencer and I wanted him to be guilty?

4

I waited for Spencer at the front of the post office so I didn't risk drawing Travis's attention again. Spencer's latest message told me his parcel seemed to have stayed put this time around, but that didn't mean it wouldn't disappear when his back was turned.

Spencer approached and greeted me with a kiss. "How'd it go?"

"Not entirely according to plan," I admitted. "Travis caught me outside when Sunbeam accidentally fell through the window and landed on him."

Sunbeam let out a sheepish hoot, while Spencer's eyes widened in alarm. "He didn't figure out why you were there, did he?"

"I convinced him I was waiting for you, and he seemed to believe me," I explained. "It's my fault. I sent Sunbeam to peer through the window because he was on his phone under the table, and I wanted to see if he was messaging someone while you were delivering the package."

"Was he?"

"I don't know, because I didn't realise the window was open until Sunbeam fell through it. If it's any consolation, Travis's expression when Sunbeam hit him was hilarious."

"I bet." A smile tugged his mouth. "At least he didn't figure out you were spying on him."

"I think he knows I suspect him of meddling with your deliveries, though. I sneaked in a couple of questions and got mostly nonanswers."

"Oh?" He raised a brow. "What did he say?"

"He called you an overachiever and implied that there weren't enough staff to handle all the deliveries."

"That part might be true," Spencer said. "As for the 'overachiever' part, though… anyone who isn't working their tail off at this time of year is seriously slacking. I told him that myself so the boss wouldn't take it out on all of us at once if we fell behind."

"I figured it was something like that," I said. "I don't get the impression he likes his job either."

"No, but I'd have thought he'd want to avoid making his own life harder by slowing down our deliveries." His expression turned preoccupied. "Unless he hoped I'd be the one to take the impact and that it wouldn't affect him at all."

"Maybe." Travis had struck me as the sort of person who stayed far away from anything that involved actual effort. How had he pulled off the package thefts without lifting a finger? "Your supervisor isn't blaming you, is he?"

"It's easier to blame an employee than go out there and find out the truth." He scowled. "No doubt that's exactly what the culprit intended."

"That's not fair," I protested. "It's obvious that you can't have transported those packages to the opposite side of town yourself."

"Dennis is rushed off his feet dealing with customer complaints already," he said. "I'm the obvious target. Unless someone exposes the real culprit, I'm going to take the blame."

Indignation rose within me. "Not on my watch. I wish I'd seen what Travis was doing on his phone, but if he's working with someone else, there's only so many people who have the type of magical skill necessary to send two massive boxes to the wrong side of town without being there in person."

"Right," he agreed. "I should head back into…"

He trailed off as the door opened and a red-faced elf wearing a green outfit trimmed in gold came out of the post office.

"Spencer!" he bellowed. "Slacking off, are you?"

"Ah—hello, Dennis," Spencer said, probably for my benefit. *That's his supervisor? He looks like a leprechaun.* "I just got back from my last delivery. I told Carol here about the missing packages…"

"Carol?" Dennis turned towards me with visible hostility in his expression. "You look familiar."

"Erm… I work at the Holiday Haven Inn." I was pretty sure I'd never met this guy before, so it was beyond me to figure out why he seemed irked. Unless he thought I was luring Spencer away from his job. At least he hadn't heard our conversation… or so I hoped.

"That place." He scoffed. "What a joke. Who goes on holiday to the North Pole?"

"Excuse me?" My hackles went up. "We get plenty of

tourists, and we've been going from strength to strength over the past six years. We're expecting at least two hundred attendees to our event this weekend."

He gave me a disbelieving look. "Then why are you here?"

"I offered to help Spencer find the missing packages," I repeated. "We frequently order things in the post, so I assumed that we were likely to be affected sooner or later. Have you looked into what's causing the packages to disappear?"

"I can tell what's causing my employee to fail to do his job." He narrowed his eyes at me. "Go home."

He had some nerve insulting my place of work. Part of me wanted to dig my heels in, but I suspected that that wouldn't help the situation for either of us.

"Spencer did nothing wrong," I told him. "I was looking after Sunbeam while he was out making deliveries."

Sunbeam hooted in agreement, but Dennis looked unimpressed with both of us.

"I heard that ridiculous creature making a racket in the post room," he said. "I thought you trained him, Spencer."

"He was looking for me," Spencer said. "He didn't do any harm. Anyway, you're welcome to check with my last customer to confirm that I made the delivery as planned. I saw him take it into the house."

That means it can't be stolen from outside, at least, I thought.

"Then come inside and stop wasting time." Dennis stalked back into the building while I gaped after him.

"Wow."

ELLE ADAMS

"Yeah… that's the boss," Spencer murmured. "Sorry about him."

"His reaction was a bit much," I remarked. "You'd think I'd stolen the packages myself. Also, what *is* his problem with the Holiday Haven Inn? Does he have something against tourists?"

"No… I think he had a bad experience at Janice's inn once, though. I'll have to ask him."

"That's no reason to tar all of us with the same brush," I said. "I've had plenty of bad experiences with her too."

I wondered what she'd done to annoy him so much. Then again, he seemed the type who'd find something to complain about even if the service was perfect, so perhaps it was for the best that he'd stayed at Janice's inn and not ours. It didn't give him the right to bad-mouth us behind our backs, though.

"I know he's being irrational." He reached out and took my hand. "He's under a ton of stress right now, but that's no excuse for his behaviour."

"You definitely saw the customer take the delivery into the house?" I asked. "I'm assuming that means it's not going to be possible for anyone to steal it, right?"

"I'd like to hope so," he said. "Honestly, I can't picture someone striding up and picking up that rocking horse single-handedly even from outside, though. If magic is involved, it's another issue entirely."

"Exactly." I glanced over at the building, from which several owls had taken flight with packages gripped in their claws. "You'd better get back inside before the leprechaun comes back."

He choked on a laugh. "You aren't the only one who

calls him that... not to his face, though. I'll give you an update if there's any other developments."

Spencer went back into the office while I pondered Dennis's attitude problem and wondered just what Janice had done to offend him so much. I didn't think even Janice would have set out to make his experience at her inn unpleasant. She wanted to keep her business afloat as much as Mercy and I did.

That's a question for another day.

In the meantime, I walked back to the inn, hoping I hadn't screwed up by attracting so much attention at the post office. Now both Travis and Dennis knew I'd taken an interest in the missing packages, and I might have unintentionally made it harder to prove Travis was the culprit as a result. On the other hand, maybe he'd give it a rest now that he knew he was being watched. You never knew.

Mercy gave me an odd look when I walked into the reception area. "There you are. Why is there an owl on your head?"

"Huh?" I opened my coat, and Sunbeam flew out of the hood, making me jump. "I guess he followed me home. He might as well stay here for the time being, since the boss isn't happy with him."

"Whose boss?"

"Spencer's." I hung up my coat. "He doesn't like *me* much either, though I haven't a clue why. It's been a weird morning."

I told her everything that had transpired since I'd left the inn. As predicted, Mercy found the incident with Sunbeam falling through the window as amusing as I did.

"Serve that Travis right for slacking off on the job," she said. "He sounds like every bad co-worker I've had."

"The boss isn't much better," I said. "He blames Spencer for his packages vanishing, as if he could have had anything to do with it. To top it off, he insulted our inn too."

"He did *what?*"

I grimaced. "According to Spencer, Dennis had a bad experience with Janice, of all people, a while ago, so he's decided our inn is terrible by association. He claimed that tourists don't come to town, so it's a waste of time."

"Well, that's utter nonsense," she said. "Maybe tourists don't order mail, but they certainly come to Holiday Haven. I've been fielding calls from people wanting to book in for the Christmas period all morning."

"I know," I said. "He wouldn't let me get a word in edgeways back then, but I wish I'd said more in our favour. He seemed predisposed to hate us on principle. It's not our fault Janice was terrible at customer service."

Sunbeam hooted in agreement from his new perch atop the Christmas tree in the corner.

Mercy pursed her lips. "I wonder what she did to annoy him so much."

"I doubt she'll tell us, and he certainly won't," I said. "Anyway, is it okay if Sunbeam hangs out here until Spencer gets back? His boss wasn't happy with him over the window incident, which was more my fault than his, so I figure he should lie low for a bit."

"Sure," she replied. "We could always use a happy baby owl to keep us entertained."

"He's not really a baby anymore, though." My gaze followed Sunbeam as he tapped on a bauble with his beak, its reflective surface showing his huge owl-eyes. "I think he's always going to be a miniature owl."

"Cute."

Sunbeam hooted happily, no worse for wear from the criticism the boss had levelled at him about not being fit for the job. I was willing to bet he worked harder than Travis did, at the very least.

"Speaking of Janice," I added, "have you found out her schedule for this weekend's event yet?"

"Not yet, but I haven't got outside today," she replied. "I'm waiting for updates from Daryl on rehearsals."

"Oh yeah," I said. "Is everyone okay? The ones who don't have flu, I mean?"

"So far, but they're going to be cutting it fine with the rehearsals," she said. "They might have to do the dress rehearsal at the studio instead of here. That okay?"

"Sure. They already know their way around the stage from last year, so it's no big deal." At least we'd avoid a repeat of the frog incident. And the part when the tinsel had turned into snakes and Daryl had ended up getting bitten.

Hmm. After last year, it was no wonder the notion of half the theatre group having flu didn't bug me too much. Unlike the idea of someone trying to ruin the holidays *and* get my boyfriend into trouble with his supervisor over his missing packages.

"As for the rest of it…" She held up the notebook in which we'd written down the event's schedule. "The carollers will be ready to rehearse later. I'll let you know what time when I hear from Larry."

"Sure, that won't be an issue."

The only guest around was Gerry, and he wouldn't

mind listening to the carollers rehearse downstairs at the inn. Meanwhile, I went into the hall to put up the new decorations I'd made to replace the tinsel from yesterday —namely, a few paper owls which may have been based on a certain someone I knew. Sunbeam flew into the hall to watch and hooted his approval as I climbed the ladder and fixed each paper owl to the wall. Once a row of wide-eyed owls watched us from the walls, I used my magic to add a sparkling touch to their wings.

"There we go." I stepped down off the ladder. "What do you think, Sunbeam?"

He hooted happily and flew in circles while Mercy came into the hall behind me. "Are you talking to yourself?"

"No, I'm talking to Sunbeam." Mostly to stop my thoughts from drifting towards Spencer and the myste-rious package thief, admittedly, but it'd worked. "What do you think of those owls?"

"Perfect." Mercy's eyes followed Sunbeam's progress as he flew around the ceiling. "We could have asked some owls to volunteer to be part of our show. A display of synchronised owls in flight would have been a fun addi-tion to our schedule."

"True, but can you imagine cleaning up the mess afterwards?"

My phone buzzed. *Spencer.* It'd been an hour or so since I'd left him at the post office. Had the package already disappeared?

I left the hall with the phone in my hand and answered the call. "Hey. Good news or bad?"

"Both."

"Oh boy. Tell me the worst."

"The bad news is that our serial prankster has struck again," he answered. "The good news? I wasn't the victim this time."

"Wait, you weren't?" I asked, disarmed.

"Nope," he replied. "Everyone on my shift is complaining of packages switching themselves with others. It's complete chaos in here."

"Oh, no," I said. "I bet Dennis isn't pleased."

"That's an understatement. I barely got away in time to call you." He lowered his voice. "I'm afraid I probably won't be able to drop by the inn this evening if I'm going to spend the rest of the day redelivering packages."

"I'm glad it's not just you who's being affected."

"Might have been easier to solve if it was," he said. "The boss is coming—I'll update you later."

He ended the call while I stared at the phone. *It's not just him.* Either Travis had gone to extreme lengths to hide his trail, or something more was at work than a simple grudge. For the entire postal service to be screwed up just before the holiday season suggested someone was set on ruining the fun for everyone in town.

How had they pulled off something of this magnitude, though? Was it all intended or at random? If the former, then I had to wonder if this situation was caused by someone with connections, someone who knew where all the packages would be delivered and therefore how to switch them around for maximum chaos. My mind briefly landed on Dennis. That guy was a grinch if I ever saw one, but he was in charge of the post office and wouldn't want it sabotaged. I'd been inclined to dislike him after he'd set himself against our inn for no reason whatsoever, but that didn't mean he was in any way responsible.

All the same, I didn't see someone as lazy as Travis pulling off this complicated a scheme. And if Spencer was going to be run off his feet all day fixing the damage, then someone else needed to find the culprit.

5

"Who'd want to screw up the entire postal system?" I remarked to Mercy once I'd put down my phone. "Or should that be 'How did they screw it up?'"

Her brow wrinkled. "What's actually going on? Someone's stealing packages?"

"They're vanishing and then showing up at the wrong addresses," I said. "Maybe someone tried a Secret Santa spell and it got screwed up somewhere."

"Is that a thing?" she asked.

"Haven't a clue." I heaved a sigh. "I'm trying to think of anyone who has the magical clout to pull off something this big and drawing a blank."

"Yeah... I have no idea." She glanced over at the stairs at the sound of footsteps from the upper floor.

A moment later, Gerry came wandering into the reception area and gave a dramatic flourish before pulling two playing cards out of thin air. "Did I hear someone mention magic?"

"Not that kind of magic." I wasn't entirely certain whether he was just a stage magician or if he had an actual gift of his own, but since he lived in his own little world, I had my doubts that he'd even noticed anything weird was going on.

"Oh." The two playing cards he'd pulled out of nowhere disappeared into his sleeves. "Never mind. Can I borrow three spoons? I need them for a new trick."

"Sure, why not." At this point I'd learned not to blink at his weird demands. It was hardly odder than how I'd spent my morning, after all. "I'll send them up to your room."

———

Just after lunchtime, my phone buzzed with another call from Spencer.

"Hey, there," I answered. "How's it going?"

"Hectic," he replied. "We've had to split into two teams —one to field complaints and give directions and the other to actually redeliver all the packages. Some of them are unaccounted for, so I assume they're lagging a bit and will reappear later."

"Hope so," I said. "I'm still trying to figure out what kind of spell caused this. It can't be anything else, but I honestly have no idea."

"Neither does anyone else," he said. "Whatever spell it is, it's far too wide-ranging to be a simple enchantment. So far, it's only hitting Holiday Haven, but I don't know what'll happen if it moves to the central North Pole as well."

I winced at the thought of that level of disruption, not

to mention how irked Santa and his wife would be if their own holiday plans ended up in disarray. "I hope the spell stops before it gets to that stage."

"Same," he said. "Also, you won't believe the last person who called to make a complaint about a missing package. Janice."

"Janice?" I echoed, seeing Mercy give me a sideways look. "What did she order?"

"She didn't say," he said. "I had to handle her complaint, and I could barely get a word in edgeways. I'm not even responsible for her order, or for the one it got switched with, but I said I'd take it to her as soon as it showed up. I figured you wanted to know."

"Are you going to ask what she did to annoy your boss while you're at it?" I glanced over at Mercy, who mouthed, *Go with him.* She must have figured out the situation without me having to say anything. "Tell you what, I can come with you. I'll bring Sunbeam... I assume you know he followed me back to the inn."

"Are you sure?" he asked. "You aren't an employee, so the boss might not be thrilled if he catches you—though he's a bit distracted at the moment."

"I won't stick around the office for long," I told him. "He can't complain if I offer to help carry Janice's package to her. I assume he doesn't want to deal with her if they have an unpleasant history."

"No, but I can't say I know what it is."

"Nor me, but I'd also like to know what she ordered," I said. "Mercy and I are sure she's planning to rip off our event this weekend, but neither of us has had the chance to snoop around."

"Well... all right," he said. "Meet you in half an hour?"

"Sure." After the call ended, I faced Mercy. "Will you be okay without me for an hour or so?"

"Of course," she said. "Try not to provoke Janice unnecessarily, though. We don't need her retaliating and messing up our event even more than it already is."

"True." Unless… might *she* be behind our current spate of misfortune? It wasn't the first time I'd suspected her of making trouble and been mistaken, though, and she seemed to have been one of the victims of the package trickery herself. I put the thought out of mind for now. "I do want to know what she did to Dennis when he stayed at her inn."

"I'm more interested in what she's planning this weekend," she said. "I swear, if she copied our schedule and menu again… Are you sure she won't get mad at you for sneaking around her inn?"

"I'm not sneaking around. I'm doing her a favour," I said. "She can't complain if I bring her missing package, can she?"

"I guess not," she relented. "Wait. If the spell is affecting all the deliveries, I have one of my own due to arrive this afternoon."

"Uh-oh." I beckoned Sunbeam over to me. "If it goes missing and reappears elsewhere, we'll bring it straight back. I'll ask Spencer."

"Thanks." She flashed me a weak smile. "Just another day at the inn, right?"

"Exactly." I grabbed my coat and shoes before leaving for the post office yet again.

Sunbeam flew at my side down the snow-laden streets, while this time I waited out of sight of the doors *and* the windows of the post office, not wanting to take any chances.

Within a minute, Spencer came out to meet us. "Don't worry, Dennis isn't paying any attention to anything except customer demands at the moment."

"And Travis?"

"He's chasing down packages. Like everyone else, pretty much." He gave a satisfied nod. "He has no time for his usual slacking off, so if he's responsible for this, then he's landed himself in a pile of stress as well as the rest of us."

"Serve him right," I said. "Where's Janice's package?"

"In there." He indicated the door to the office building. "It's easier for two of us to carry it, so I doubt anyone will complain about you giving me a hand. I'll grab some other smaller packages so I can deliver those on the way back."

"Good call." I tensed when he opened the door, but nobody looked up from their small mountains of packages and envelopes. I followed him tentatively, one eye on the offices at the back.

"Relax, the boss isn't around," he said. "He's on the phone, trying to find someone to complain to about the mix-up, not very successfully. Everyone else is blaming him, or the post office as a whole."

Hmm. Maybe Travis had found it worth inconveniencing himself just for a shot at annoying the boss, but if so, he'd definitely taken it too far.

Spencer crouched down beside the large square box Janice had ordered, and I helped him lift it into the air. He did most of the work, since my job at the inn didn't typically involve lifting heavy objects and I didn't have much in the way of upper-body strength. Neither did Sunbeam, who contributed by taking some of the smaller envelopes from the desk while Spencer and I manoeuvred the package through the front door.

Carrying the large box down the snowy street was even trickier. We had to turn around so that Spencer walked backwards, since he was slightly less likely to fall on his face than I was. As a result, I had to warn him of any upcoming obstacles as we veered towards Janice's inn.

"What *is* in here?" I puffed out, my arms aching from the effort of holding the box. "Bricks?"

"No… theatre props, I think," he replied. "Stuff for her event."

"Oh, boy." As we neared Janice's inn, I spied a very familiar display of snow witches outside the doors. She'd also installed a new sign which read "Merry Christmas" in glittering letters, and I was willing to bet it changed themes depending on the holiday the same way our own sign did. "I swear, if she copied our schedule again…"

"Want me to talk to her?"

"Nah, this is why I volunteered to come. We'll talk face-to-face."

I never quite knew what to expect with Janice, but since we'd been civil to one another over the last few months, I hoped she'd be in a reasonable mood. Though now I thought about it, perhaps showing up with her missing delivery hadn't been my smartest idea. Blaming me for her own misfortune was her go-to strategy, but it was too late to turn back now.

Sure enough, her eyes flew wide when she spotted me through the transparent doors to the inn. Spencer walked backwards ahead of me, and the doors slid open, letting us carry the box through into the reception area.

Janice goggled at us. "What are *you* doing here?"

"Delivering your package. You're welcome."

I helped Spencer put down the box and then turned to face my sort-of-nemesis. She looked as if she'd seen a ghost, which seemed a bit of an overreaction to my presence—and which instantly drew my suspicions.

When she didn't reply, I added, "Some jokester has decided it's funny to switch everyone's presents around."

"I assumed you were screwing around with that magic box again."

"I—" The wishing box? Why would she even bring that up? "No, we aren't. We have more sense. Why would we even use it to mess with people's mail, anyway?"

She made a sceptical noise. "You kept it, didn't you? From last year."

"Okay, this is not my doing." I'd expected her to find a way to blame me for her missing delivery, but the possibility of her bringing up the wishing box hadn't even been on my radar. "I have an event to run. I don't have time to mess around with wishes."

"You had time to come here." She scooted out from behind the counter to examine the box from a distance, as if it contained a live scorpion.

"It's fine," I told her. "Honest."

"I hope it doesn't mysteriously disappear again, then." Turning to Spencer, she added, "If you have someone pranking your post office, it sounds like you need to get rid of an employee or two."

"It might not be an employee." I watched her face, trying to gauge her reaction. "Given the scale, it's got to be someone with access to magic."

"I don't know what you expect me to say to that," she

said. "You have magic, not me. Oh, and you might want to check that box of yours to see if it's where it's supposed to be."

"It isn't the wishing box." I hadn't even looked at it in months, though Mercy and I had always planned to pull it out again for our event this year. Last time we'd had to lay out strict rules and check before putting each wish into the box, and we fully intended on doing the same again.

She scowled. "Look, you're a troublemaker. It's a fact."

"It isn't Carol's fault," Spencer put in. "Is there anywhere else you want us to take the box? Like the hall?"

I followed his gaze towards the door at the back of the reception area, which must lead to the hall Janice would be using for her own event.

"Why are you being nice to me?" She looked between us, her expression haughty. "You're up to something."

"I'm doing my job," said Spencer simply. "If you want to carry the box yourself, then you're welcome to."

I hid a smile while her jaw twitched. "Go on, then. Get on with it."

We picked up the box again while I wondered what her issue could possibly be. Maybe it was just that she couldn't see any favour as anything other than an attack, which was kind of sad, but as for her comments about the wishing box… The chaos at the post office could theoretically be caused by a wish gone wrong, but I didn't think anyone else in town owned one at all.

Mercy and I had left ours untouched since last year, and while I'd come close to breaking my resolution during last summer's chaotic events, I was glad I'd held off. Everything had ultimately worked out in the end, and in my experience, wishes couldn't solve everyone's problems and were more likely to cause new ones than not.

Once we'd gone through the door, Spencer and I put down the box carefully in front of a large stage. Chairs lined the wooden floor, where tinsel hung from the wall. Annoyingly, Janice's tinsel seemed to have stayed attached to the walls rather than falling down the way ours had, though I happened to think the owls I'd made as an alternative were nicer than her own décor.

Regardless, it couldn't be more obvious that she'd borrowed her design from our own stage the previous year. I scanned the hall and spotted a piece of paper affixed to the back of the door, giving the schedule of the event. *A play, carollers, entertainment...*

My heart dropped when I took in the date. She planned to start a day earlier than ours: on Friday instead of Saturday. And if she *had* borrowed our schedule down to the minute, would the townspeople really want to watch the exact same show two days in a row?

I looked up sharply when a creaking noise came from the back of the hall, and a door was nudged open. Someone peered through and then withdrew so swiftly they left little more than a blur on my eyelids. I could only be sure of one thing... the person who'd looked into the hall had wings.

"Did you see what I just did?" I whispered to Spencer.

"That was fast." He eyed the door. "Who were they?"

"I think," I murmured, "it was a fairy."

"What are you two doing in there?" Janice's voice drifted through the door from the reception area. "Nosing around?"

I didn't quite have the nerve to go chasing after her

guest, and they'd moved so fast that I might not catch them anyway. Instead, I left the hall and approached the front desk. "I see you changed up the schedule."

"And?" A challenging note entered her voice.

"And nothing." I recalled Gerry's comment about trying to book a room at Janice's inn and finding no vacancies, but all I could think about was that flutter of wings I'd seen. "Do you have a lot of guests at the moment?"

"Yes. Why is that a surprise?"

"It isn't." Someone was touchy today. "One of my guests mentioned trying to book a room at your inn and finding it full up, that's all."

A smirk flitted onto her mouth. "Sore about being second best?"

"Not in the least," I said evenly. "I have a question. Did Dennis ever stay at the inn?"

"Who?"

"A supervisor at the post office. He's an elf who dresses like a leprechaun. I imagine you remember him."

A flush spread over her cheeks. "I don't see how it's any of your business."

"Just curious," I said innocently. "Something he said to me earlier implied he had experience with your inn. Not a pleasant one either."

Her jaw twitched. "Get out."

Okay, maybe I'd hoped for too much when I'd come in here wanting her to answer some of my burning questions, but I'd left with a whole new set of queries *and* the knowledge that Mercy and I needed to make some quick decisions if we didn't want Janice to steal our event from under our feet.

"I guess it was a long shot," I murmured to Spencer when the door closed behind us. "That she'd tell me what she did to Dennis, I mean. It's as likely that he made up something to complain about as not."

"You aren't wrong," he said. "I see what you meant about her attitude, though. Is it even legal for her to copy your event schedule?"

"Our event isn't copyrighted, so yes." I sighed. "Mercy is going to freak out. I don't know that we can plan a do-over this close to the time."

"Relax." He wrapped an arm around me. "Your schedule isn't an exact match. You have some things she doesn't, right?"

"Yeah... the wishing box," I said. "And my parents' hats. She can't come up with anything like that, but I wish we'd mixed up the rest."

"It'll be fine." He glanced behind us. "She's nothing but a pale imitation. I can't believe she even copied your signpost."

"Yeah." I tilted my head, spying the little owl perched on the signpost. "Sunbeam, can you have a look upstairs and see if you can spot a fairy in any of the rooms? Please don't sit on the window this time, though."

He squeaked agreement, took flight to the upper level of the inn, and peered through each window one at a time. After he'd circled the building, he flew back down and shook his little head.

"Guess the fairy flew off," I concluded. "I didn't know there was one in town."

"I didn't either," said Spencer. "I only see people I deliver packages to, and I can't say I make a habit of stopping at Janice's inn. Looked like the fairy is a guest, not part of the event, though."

"I didn't even think of that."

Whenever anyone mentioned fairies, I had a hard time not thinking of a certain group of guests who'd come to stay at the inn over the summer. If Janice was working one step ahead of us, had she gone to more extreme measures to show us up and ensure her event surpassed ours? Measures like hiring a fairy with the same abilities as the last one we'd hosted.

If her attitude was anything to go by, her grudge was alive and well, but she wouldn't use wishes against us, surely.

Right?

6

"What did Janice do this time?" Mercy wanted to know when I returned to the inn.

"She moved up her event so it starts a day before ours," I replied. "And copied our schedule, but we already guessed she'd do that."

"No." She sat down so abruptly on the chair behind the desk that for a moment I thought she'd fallen onto the floor. "This is a disaster."

"It's not the end of the world," I reassured her. "She doesn't have the wishing box or my parents' hats. She copied the bare bones of our event, but we have far more than she does."

"I should have varied the theme," she said with a groan. "You were right."

"No." I shook my head. "If we'd strayed too far from the holiday theme, we'd have had trouble selling tickets at all. I think people would be happy to go to both our event *and* Janice's."

"Not if she tires them out or otherwise puts them off on Friday," she said. "Was she really smug about it?"

"She seems to think we're still bitter enemies," I said. "She also blamed *me* for the package situation, as well as laughing at me for Gerry's comment about wanting to stay at her inn instead of ours."

"Wow." She blinked. "I'm surprised she has a full house of guests. She must have done some aggressive marketing."

"Or made lofty promises she can't keep,'" I suggested. "When Spencer and I took her package in, she had a sort of shifty look on her face as if she'd been caught stealing from a bank vault."

"Guilty conscience?" she suggested.

"Yeah, but I'm not sure why." I racked my mind and came up with nothing. "She doesn't seem to be involved with the missing packages. Not directly, at any rate."

"Maybe she hoped we wouldn't find out she copied our schedule again." She sighed. "It's wishful thinking, hoping she'll end up in dire straits before the event starts, isn't it?"

"Probably." I paused for a moment. "Did you know she had a fairy staying at her inn?"

"A fairy?" she echoed. "Like the Fairy Godmother? Or Cupid?"

"I don't think it was either of them, nor the Tooth Fairy either. Whoever it was, they ran off as soon as they saw Spencer and me in the hall. Or flew off. Fast."

"That's… bizarre."

"Tell me about it," I said. "I don't *think* the fairy is connected to her event, but you never know."

"With her, anything is possible."

"Yeah." Odds were, the fairy wasn't a relation of any of the fairies I'd met… but why had they run away from us? "It can't be one of the fairies we know, but if they're a relation of one of them, then it's weird that they'd pick Janice's inn to stay at and not ours."

"I thought we ended our last visit on a good note," she said. "Also, we have vacancies at our own inn. Up until your parents get here, anyway. I guess the fairy might have wanted to stay longer…"

"Might be for the best that we don't have fairies staying here as well as my parents." All the same, my visit to Janice had left me with a new stack of questions to add to the mystery of whatever she'd done to make an enemy of Dennis. "Don't get too fussed over the event, though. There's nothing we can do now."

"Maybe there is." She paced around the desk. "It's not too late to switch around the schedule."

"Like what?" I asked. "The theatre group isn't putting on the exact same play as hers, I'm sure. And there are only so many Christmas carols to go around."

"I'll have a think." Her brow scrunched up. "Or we can move up the timetable by a day, so we start at the same time after all."

"No, that'll just stress everyone out," I said. "I'm more concerned with why Janice thinks I'm plotting against her."

"Like I said, it's a guilty conscience," Mercy said firmly. "We haven't spoken to her in months. Whatever she's concluded is all in her head."

"Exactly." The more I thought on it, the more suspicious I grew that she'd given us a reason to plot against her without either of us even knowing it. "I guess I'll have to find another excuse to pay her a visit. Maybe her package will disappear again."

My phone buzzed. I grabbed it, expecting Spencer, but instead found another message from Mum announcing that she'd decided to bring some extra hats.

I paused on the brink of replying. Did I want to clue them in to the situation? Probably not, given that they tended to bring enough chaos along with them without adding our own on top of it. Though the issues at the post office might impact their upcoming meeting with Spencer, if he couldn't get away from work this weekend after all. As for Janice... it might be amusing to watch my parents give her a talking-to as they'd done last year, but I really thought we were past this.

The same went for her accusations about us using the wishing box, for that matter. I decided not to mention that part, not even to Mercy. She was stressed already, and it would only invite unnecessary distractions. Janice was being paranoid, nothing more.

Yet I couldn't help wondering if part of her theory had merit. Had the chaos at the post office resulted from a misapplied wish, and if so, who was responsible? Or had it been intentional? I didn't know, but Mercy's dark expression suggested her mind was ticking with unpleasant theories too. When it started to snow, I turned towards her. "Mercy, I know I told you to chill out, but this isn't what I had in mind."

"Sorry." She lowered her hand, bringing a sweep of snowflakes to the floor. "I was just... lost in thought."

"I know what you mean." On a whim, I replied to Mum's text message with a brief explanation of Janice's attempt to undercut us. No need to mention the package mix-up, but I could at least prepare my parents for the possibility that everyone would be too busy at Janice's inn on Friday to buy any of their hats.

At that moment, Gerry came walking downstairs, singing, "Let it snow, let it snow, let it snow."

"Hey, Gerry," I said to him.

"Would you look at that." He beamed around him at the snowflakes glittering in the air. "I really do have the magic touch."

I decided not to tell him the snow was Mercy's doing. "Anything I can help you with?"

He lowered his head. "Sorry, I lost your spoons."

"You… lost them?"

He nodded gravely. "I was trying a disappearing spell, and they never came back."

"Does that happen often?" With Gerry, it was anyone's guess as to whether he'd meant they'd vanished in a literal sense or not.

"Sometimes," he said. "They might show up again."

I glanced at Mercy, whose expression of bafflement mirrored my own. "I'll tell the kitchen staff. I'm sure they won't mind."

"Things can get lost between realities surprisingly easily," he told me. "With magic, anything is possible."

Okay… "You know a lot about magic? Erm, the not-stagey stuff?"

"I dabble." A rabbit popped its head out of his sleeve and withdrew again. "You've meddled with reality yourself before, haven't you?"

"Meddled with reality?" Maybe I should have ended this conversation before it started. "I have a magical gift, but not a strong one."

ELLE ADAMS

"But you've touched something stronger." He nodded sagely. "Something with the power to move objects between realities. There are always rules to magic, and if you run up against its limitations..." He snapped his fingers. Nothing happened, but apparently that was intentional, because he gave a satisfied smile.

Gerry wandered off before I could answer, leaving me blinking after him. He couldn't have meant the wishing box, could he? We hadn't mentioned the subject in front of him, as far as I was aware, but conjuring objects out of nothing might count as meddling with reality. Or he might be talking nonsense.

Unless he did know something I didn't. Let's face it, I wouldn't know the first thing about the actual mechanics of the wishing box. And if someone in town had used a similar spell to cause the current madness at the post office, he might have picked up on it. That didn't mean Gerry, of all people, was responsible, though. He was too busy disappearing our spoons. Shoving the thought out of mind, I checked my phone and found another message from my parents... this one offering to arrive a day earlier than planned.

Should I say yes? If they arrived early, we'd have at least part of our event ready in advance of Janice's scheming, but what were the odds of finding the person responsible for the post office chaos before then? Not to mention Spencer would be busy the whole time and might not get to meet them at all.

No. I hadn't expended all this energy and time setting up the visit only for it to crash and burn, so I doubled my resolution to help solve the mystery. Wiping the snow Mercy had conjured off the desk with my sleeve, I said, "I

66

told my parents about Janice, and they offered to fly in tomorrow instead."

She blinked. "To do what?"

"To stop Janice overtaking us, if possible," I replied. "I think. They didn't say… and I haven't told them about the package situation yet either."

As if on cue, the door opened, and an owl flew into the reception area, dropping a package on the desk. I stared at it for a moment, an idea occurring to me. The package couldn't disappear if it had already been opened, could it? Gerry might live in his own strange world, but what he'd said about there always being rules for magic was technically true. The spell someone had used on the postal service must have limits, however little we understood them.

"Is that mine?" Mercy picked up the package. "Better open it before it disappears."

"I think opening it might break the spell," I said. "This spell must have rules, even if we don't understand what they are."

She tilted her head. "Don't tell me you got that one from Gerry."

"He's not wrong. Even if he did accidentally disappear three of our spoons."

She snorted. "Well, if you're going to do a test run, don't do it on any parcels whose contents you desperately need."

I'd figured that she wouldn't appreciate her own package being used as a guinea pig, but I could order a few things of my own to test the boundaries of the spell. So far, all the boxes that had been caught in the spell had been unopened, to my knowledge, but there might be other rules we could figure out through trial and error.

"I want to help Spencer figure out what's going on," I murmured. "If we don't solve this by the weekend, we might at least be able to minimise the damage to our own event. I can order a few things to test it on... with expedited shipping."

"Good call," she said. "We don't want packages appearing all over the inn when your parents show up."

"I don't have to say yes to them arriving early," I added. "Is it too much to ask that they show up to visit on a normal week, though?"

"No such thing," she said. "At least we don't have too many other weird guests around as well."

"Don't speak too soon. Gerry seems to be intent on disappearing our cutlery."

"He's not all there, I know." A grin tugged at her mouth. "Ask your parents to come, though. They might be able to help us out. Or at least throw another snowball at Janice like last year."

"All right." After replying to Mum's message, I went to the computer behind the desk and ordered a few things online to test out my theories on. Almost instantly I wondered if I should've checked with Spencer first to make sure I wasn't piling too much more work on the post office, so I called his number. The phone rang several times before he picked up.

"Hey, Carol," he said breathlessly. "Sorry... I had my phone in my pocket. I need to plug it in to charge soon, but I'm not getting off my shift until midnight."

"Sorry I distracted you," I said. "I just wanted to run an idea past you to see if it's okay."

"An idea?"

"Mercy's package showed up, and so far it's stuck around," I explained. "I think opening the packages might stop the spell from causing them to vanish. If there are other rules surrounding the spell, then I thought I might be able to find out what they are."

"Rules?" he asked. "I suppose it can't hurt to experiment, but for some reason the boss thinks that if we keep aggressively delivering everything over and over again, they'll eventually stick."

"I probably didn't help by ordering a few things to test my theories on," I said apologetically. "Only small packages, nothing huge."

"Nah, it's not that bad. People who insist on ordering full-sized snowmen and other impractical things are the ones causing us the most trouble."

"How would you even go about delivering a snowman?"

"It involves an ice-cold box and a lot of optimism."

"I bet." Honestly. Why order a snowman when they could just build their own? There was hardly a shortage of snow here in Holiday Haven. "I figured that if we found the limits, we might be able to stop the spell in its tracks."

"Might be tricky to convince everyone to open their presents in advance," he remarked. "Also, there are always some people who refuse to answer the door to us."

"You mean anyone antisocial who doesn't want to talk to an actual person when they collect their mail," I quipped. "Nah, I used to do that myself sometimes. But if that's the key to stopping this spell, then it might be worth the trade-off."

"You aren't wrong," he said. "I dropped the suggestion

of it being a spell to my boss earlier, actually, but he shut down the idea."

"No surprise there." Dennis hadn't exactly seemed open to listening to anyone else's ideas. Was he purposefully trying to make everyone's lives more difficult or just determined not to slow down the speed of deliveries so close to the holidays despite the obvious drawbacks to that strategy? "I have a dozen theories about what caused the spell and no evidence, so I figured it couldn't hurt to make a game plan in the meantime."

"True," he said. "We can print out instructions to customers…"

"Don't tell Dennis," I said hastily. "He'll only slow you down. Tell you what, I can design some leaflets myself with instructions printed on them. Mercy and I are already sending out leaflets for our event, so this isn't too much trouble."

"You really don't have to," he protested. "Honestly, this is our problem, not yours."

"It's all of our problem," I corrected. "Besides, I want you to be able to meet my parents this weekend, which is only possible if we sort out this mess."

"Okay, you've got me there," he said, a smile in his voice. "If you're sure."

"I am. Check back with me in a couple of hours." I opted not to tell him my parents would show up early for now, since we hadn't finalised our arrangements yet and I didn't need to add to his stress.

After ending the call, I grabbed a notebook and drew up a plan. Firstly, I listed the "rules" for the spell that I'd guessed so far—namely, that opening the packages seemed to break the pattern—and tried to think of others.

Would a package still vanish if the person didn't open it but kept it within sight? It didn't make much sense for the spell to depend on someone paying attention, since even if a person turned out to be responsible for the spell, they couldn't be in several places at once.

Before long, I found myself ruminating on the possible culprit. The spell had been active for more than a day, and if it *was* a wish, didn't they sometimes have time limits on them? The Fairy Godmother's did. Each person got three wishes per day, no more. If it wasn't her, then a wishing box was the only other solution I knew of, but I didn't know for certain a wish had caused this at all. If not for Janice's paranoia, the thought might not have crossed my mind.

Let's face it, we had far too few clues to go on, and given that we were on the second day of the spell, it was safe to say the spell wouldn't abruptly cut out at midnight like the Fairy Godmother's wishes did. Until we knew otherwise, we'd have to assume it'd go on indefinitely.

Which meant that like it or not, we had to work with the rules of the spell… or let Christmas fall into chaos.

Mercy came into the reception area as I was sketching out designs for leaflets to inform the public about changes to the delivery service. She leaned over and picked up the notepad on which I'd listed the possible culprits behind the spell. "Janice isn't at the top of the list?"

"She wouldn't be on the list at all if she hadn't implicated herself back then," I said. "Besides, Travis is still the most likely culprit. He at least has a motive."

"You mean the desire to annoy Spencer as much as possible?"

"Yeah, and he doesn't like the boss either."

"You mean Dennis... the Menace?" She snorted when she read the name. "I'm guessing people don't call him that to his face. You put him above Janice on the list."

"Only because he's being an obstructionist," I said. "According to Spencer, the boss wants to carry on as if nothing is happening, even if it wrecks the holidays and runs his people ragged."

That didn't mean he had anything to do with the situation, but he certainly wasn't helping matters by being so obstinate. Hence why I'd taken it upon myself to design various leaflets informing the public that if they didn't open their mail in a timely manner, it might end up on the other side of town.

"What are you going to do with those?" Mercy indicated the leaflet designs.

"I'll spread them around town so that everyone who's getting a delivery knows about impending disruption," I told her. "I'm sure Sunbeam is willing to help out, and he did a great job with the leaflets for our event."

"We might have to redo those if we shake up the schedule," she said. "Which is a whole new issue."

"It's doable," I reassured her. "I doubt everyone has memorised our schedule, and I can make posters and flyers with no trouble."

"I don't know…" She exhaled in a sigh. "Should we be telling everyone in town that there's a problem with the postal service? That supervisor might not like it."

"Better than keeping them in the dark," I said firmly. "Someone has sabotaged the entire holiday delivery programme, and if I was ordering anything valuable, I'd rather know the truth than be caught off guard."

Telling everyone might lead to more complaints in the short term, admittedly, but I'd run my plan by Spencer, and he'd given me the thumbs-up. Also, asking for Sunbeam's help was better than forcing his team to take time off their overstretched schedule to distribute the leaflets themselves.

"All right," she said. "I know I'm being a downer lately, but I really think I made a mistake with this event. I didn't think Janice would be underhanded enough to borrow our entire schedule and move it up a day."

"I know." Janice's newfound commitment to our rivalry made zero sense, especially as she was the one with the full house of guests, where we were mostly empty until my parents and sister showed up. "I won't make your life harder, don't worry. Are the carollers still coming over later?"

"I haven't heard from them yet," she said. "Or from Daryl, though he always turns his phone off during rehearsals. I keep expecting more bad news."

"At least they ought to already have their costumes sorted out before the post office weirdness started." But there was no telling how many more people would be affected, since pretty much everyone did their Christmas shopping online these days.

My phone buzzed, and I found, to my surprise, that Spencer was calling me again.

"Hey," I answered. "Something up?"

"You won't believe this, but Janice's package vanished again."

"What... it did?" Seriously? "Did she not open the box?"

"Apparently not," he replied. "She left it in the hall, and it seems to have vanished of its own accord."

"So... packages can vanish multiple times."

Not good at all.

"Yeah," said Spencer. "Should I try to get assigned to her again so we can find that guest of hers?"

"You think she might be involved?"

"I'm not so sure it's Travis anymore," he said in a low voice. "He's angry at how things turned out, and I think he

74

might be on the brink of storming out of the office altogether."

"That doesn't mean he didn't do it unintentionally, though." If he'd used a wishing box and made a wish to disrupt Spencer's schedule, then I could see it spiralling out of his control. Even a Fairy Godmother-style wish could have similar results. With wishes, all bets were off.

"True," he said. "I'll let you know if I get assigned to Janice again, anyway. I have a backlog to deal with before then."

"They ought to ask for more volunteers to help them out," I remarked. "Anyway, I'll see you soon."

After I ended the call, Mercy said, "Well, my package hasn't disappeared yet."

"You opened it, right?"

"Yeah… are yours coming soon?"

"Should be." My thoughts drifted back to Janice and her newly re-stolen package. If Spencer and I were assigned to redeliver it, then we'd have to tell her to actually open the box this time around to avoid a repeat performance. That is, if she didn't tell us to get lost the instant she set eyes on us. "Janice's box has vanished again. I *hope* she didn't open it first. Imagine unwrapping your Christmas presents and then having them vanish."

"At least it might deflate her a little," said Mercy. "How'd she lose the same package twice? Are you sure she's not doing this herself to make trouble?"

"Who knows." A swooping sound came from outside. "There's my first delivery."

I ran to the porch and found a single package sitting there. If the spell depended on being opened or not, then

I'd see if bringing it directly to the desk would affect whether it disappeared.

I carried the small parcel to the desk, where Mercy eyed it. "What did you even order?"

"Identical pairs of socks. You can never have too many."

She snorted. "What're you doing with that one?"

"Putting it directly in my line of sight and waiting to see if it disappears," I replied. "I already know it'll happen if I leave it unopened outside, so now we need to narrow down the criteria a little more."

I tried not to pay too much attention to the parcel, instead focusing on designing leaflets and posters while I waited for the next delivery to show up. Mercy kept coming out of the back room to check up on me, which made this difficult.

"Maybe it won't vanish if we pay it too much attention," she suggested.

"Who needs modern entertainment when you have a nice box to play with." I shook my head. "I'm turning into Charlie the cat."

She snickered. "Speaking of whom, you might have to pause your experiments when he shows up, given his hoarding habit."

"Good point." My mother's cat had a habit of collecting shiny things and hiding them, and I'd already made a mental note to keep the wishing box firmly locked away to avoid a repeat of last year. "I'll just have to figure it out before then."

Mercy peered at the box. "If you're holding it when it vanishes, might you be able to follow it?"

"What, you think that might work?" I doubted that

would be the case, but I did wonder if there were more variables I should have included in my experiments. "It wouldn't take me to the person who actually used the spell, I don't think."

"Then I wonder what's controlling their locations?"

"No clue. We'd need a list from the post office itself to figure that one out," I said. "As far as I know, all the packages that went missing turned up at the houses of other people who ordered something, so they aren't delivering themselves to people who didn't actually order something to begin with. I think. I'll ask Spencer."

The sound of sweeping wings came from outside again. Another package landed in front of the door, and this time, I opted to leave it lying on the porch instead of bringing it inside.

"The post owls are as efficient as ever, considering everything that's going on," Mercy remarked.

"Yeah, but I feel bad for giving them more work." I returned my attention to the desk—and the spot where the first package had been sitting, which was now conspicuously empty. "Mercy—it's gone."

"Wait, what?" She startled. "I didn't see it vanish."

"Nor me." My attention had been on the door. "Maybe that's the point. I'll make a note."

I also made sure to keep the second package within my line of sight on the porch as I waited for the next arrival. Maybe I ought to set a timer so I could figure out the approximate time it took packages to vanish. Given how quickly Janice's had disappeared the second time around, it couldn't be that long. Up to half an hour at most. Though I had yet to receive anyone else's mail in return. *Hmm.*

Around twenty minutes later, the second package disappeared in a blink, to be replaced by nothing at all. Stranger and stranger.

The third package, I opened but left in the back room, out of sight. When I checked back on it later, it was still there.

"So it's true—if you open the package, you break the spell," I concluded. "Mercy, do we have any packages outside that don't belong to us yet?"

"Good question." She paced to the door and pushed it open. "Did you order a life-size cutout of Bigfoot?"

"Definitely not." When had that appeared? More to the point, what were we supposed to do with it? "I'll call the post office... though I might as well go through Spencer instead."

His boss would not be amused by my experiments. Especially as so far, I'd only confirmed what I already knew. Namely, that opening the packages broke the spell. *Right. We definitely need to get those leaflets out there.*

"Agreed," said Mercy. "I don't want that thing sitting around the inn."

"Oops," I said. "I think I'd have been better off grilling potential suspects instead. That would have been more useful."

"Don't give up just yet." Mercy lifted her head. "You never know, Spencer might be on track to figure out what caused it. I'm sure the post staff are looking into it as well, since they have to deal with the fallout."

"If they have any time."

Maybe I'd made a mistake in starting up my own experiments, but the entire *town* was involved at this point, and it sounded as if Dennis had outright refused to let his own employees do anything other than plough ahead with the same old strategies.

My phone buzzed with a new message from Spencer. *Found Janice's package. Are you in?*

Sure, I replied, figuring that I might be able to get some answers in this time around. Or find out who that fairy was at the very least.

"Where are you going?" asked Mercy.

I grabbed my coat. "To deliver Janice's mail... again."

"I bet she'll be thrilled," she commented. "Hey, if it *is* her doing this, then maybe she made it vanish on purpose just to screw with you."

"If that's true, her face will give it away as soon as I get there."

I wasn't too sure on that one, though. I'd assumed she actually wanted the delivery to show up in time for her event, but the fact that she maintained our grudge without my knowledge meant I didn't really know what she was thinking at all.

No, there'd been more behind her accusations than an old rivalry, and it was time to learn what that was.

8

Once again, Spencer met me outside the post office with Janice's delivery.

"This time it appeared across the road from her inn," he told me. "Makes a change from having to trek back and forth across town."

"Wish it'd appeared at our inn instead," I remarked. "Instead we got someone's life-sized cutout of Bigfoot."

He blinked. "Instead of what?"

"Socks. I ordered several small packages to test the spell's limits, like I told you I would."

"Ah." The confusion cleared from his expression. "What did you learn?"

"That they can disappear even from right in front of my nose, but opening the packages seems to solve the issue."

"I've found the same thing," he said. "The switching happens pretty fast too. Up until Janice, we weren't sure if it could happen to the same person twice..."

"But now we know it can. It's like a version of Secret Santa where nobody gets what they asked for."

He grinned. "You aren't wrong. That might even be the source of the spell."

"You think someone wanted to give everyone a Christmas surprise and botched the spell?" That would remove Travis from the suspect list, considering the guy struck me as the sort of person who'd utterly ignore his Secret Santa recipient and probably run off with all the presents instead. "I guess if a wish was involved, it's possible."

"I don't know about wishing boxes," he said. "To be honest, it seems more like someone's actively trying to make trouble instead."

"Like Janice," I said. "She thinks *I'm* responsible, though, which is ridiculous. She's the one who might have a fairy as a guest."

"Exactly," he said. "Let's hope we can get her to stop for a chat this time."

"Janice or the guest?" I reached down to help him pick up the box, staggering a little as he lifted the other end.

"Either," he puffed out, "but I hope she actually opens the box this time around. If not, we might have to do it for her."

With the box balanced between us, I walked backwards with Spencer steering the way to make a change. At least focusing on not falling over took my mind off everything else.

"How's the event prep going?" he asked me.

"Mercy wasn't happy to find out Janice has jumped ahead of our schedule," I replied. "As expected. Her own parcel didn't vanish after she opened it, so I don't think that's going to be an issue."

"Good," he said. "It's the people who left their Christmas shopping until the last minute who're going to have a problem."

"That reminds me," I said. "If this is caused by a wish, there's a difference between the sort granted by the Fairy Godmother and the sort you make using a wishing box. The former only lasts until midnight of that day."

"Oh," he said. "You know, though... this actually started yesterday."

"Yeah... I guess the person can keep making the same wish if needed," I said. "If the person granting the wish lets them, which I don't see the Fairy Godmother doing. She wouldn't want to ruin Christmas for everyone."

"It's something to keep in mind," he said. "My boss is utterly refusing to listen to any of my theories, though."

"Has he considered putting warning labels on the packages or otherwise sending out the news around town so that everyone knows there are delays?"

"No, that would require actually listening to one of us."

I pulled a face. "Aside from him, would anyone else be unhappy if I were to print off a bunch of posters or leaflets informing the public that they have to open their mail right away or else it'll vanish?"

"Not that I know of," he replied. "That's actually a really smart idea. If we could spare the manpower to distribute them..."

"I thought about sending Sunbeam, like I did with the leaflets for our event. He sold us a hundred tickets in an hour."

"I forgot he did that," he said. "Good idea. If it isn't too much trouble for you, that is."

"It isn't," I insisted. "Besides, I bet Sunbeam will enjoy having something useful to do, and if everyone in town knows what's going on, they might give you less grief."

"True," he acknowledged. "It's worth a shot."

"I want to solve this," I told him. "My parents have decided to come a day early so we can kick off the hat sales before Janice distracts everyone."

His brows rose. "I wish I could guarantee I'll be there to meet them, but given how things are going..."

"Don't worry. I know it's not your fault, and they'll understand."

I wish. I had to admit I was tempted to pull out the wishing box for the first time in a while, but that would be more likely to backfire than not. My family would certainly add a new layer of chaos when they showed up, but they might be able to help me find the solution too. They'd helped us pull through last year, after all.

Spencer and I neared Janice's inn, at which point I slowed down to walk backwards through the door.

"You again?" Janice said from behind me. "What are you doing here?"

"How did you manage to lose the same package twice?" I asked over my shoulder as we walked in. "If I were you, I'd open it before it vanishes again."

"I didn't ask for your advice," she returned. "Let me guess... you offered to come here to gloat at me."

"Wrong." I manoeuvred the package sideways with Spencer steering so we could carry it into the hall again. "Seriously, you're better off opening it first if you don't want it to disappear again. Unless you want me to do it instead."

"So you can steal my ideas?"

I nearly tripped over my own feet, laughing in disbelief. "Seriously? I'm not the one suffering from a lack of originality here."

I might regret those words later, but she had some nerve accusing *me* of stealing her ideas.

Spencer cleared his throat. "May I open the package, then? The spell affecting the mail seems to stop when a package is opened, so unless you want us to have to come back again…"

"Fine," she fumed, marching out from behind the desk. "I'll do it myself."

Spencer and I carried the package the rest of the way into the hall, where we set it down in the same spot as before. The instant the box touched the ground, Janice swooped in and all but shunted us backwards through the door.

As we backed into the reception area, I spied movement on the stairs nearby. Wings fluttered, and their owner made no sound as she fluttered into view. When she saw me looking, the fairy withdrew from sight with a frightened squeak.

"Whoa." I approached the stairs. "Sorry… didn't mean to startle you. If you want to come down here, go ahead."

I hadn't been mistaken. She *was* a fairy, but not the Fairy Godmother or any of the others I knew. I'd never seen her before, but the way she shrank away from me suggested she was terrified out of her mind.

"Excuse me?" I called to her. "Have we met?"

The fairy vanished in a flutter of wings, while the door

to the hall slammed and Janice reappeared with a glower on her face. "What are you doing to my guests?"

"Nothing," I said to her. "I certainly didn't do anything, but she seemed terrified. Why?"

"Stay away from my guests. You made your delivery, now get out."

"No need to be rude."

I definitely needed to talk to the fairy myself and find out what the problem was, but not here. I'd need to get her away from Janice first. In the meantime, Spencer and I left the inn.

"Weird," I murmured. "I did wonder if she might be a relation of the Fairy Godmother, but I don't understand why she picked Janice's inn over ours."

"Who knows," he said. "But you'll have a hell of a job getting past her to ask her guests questions with the mood she's in."

"I don't understand what brought this on. We literally haven't spoken in months."

"Losing her package twice couldn't have helped," said Spencer. "I'll try to drop by the inn later, but it might have to wait until tomorrow instead. When will your parents get here?"

"They told me they'd be here by late afternoon, which probably means they'll show up first thing in the morning." I gave an eye-roll. "I don't know that I should have said yes to them coming early, since I doubt they want to see the chaos going on at the moment."

"At least they won't be ordering anything in the post while they're here."

"Good point," I said. "I don't mind when you come

over to meet them. Whenever is more convenient for you."

"I'll message you and let you know when I'm free... assuming my phone's battery holds out, anyway." He kissed me goodbye and departed, while I went back to the inn with the fervent but flagging hope that this would be over before my parents showed up.

Sunbeam sat waiting on the signpost outside the inn when I got back. According to Mercy, he'd tried to help two other post owls remove the giant cardboard Bigfoot but had been unable to lift it himself.

"I have a job for you, Sunbeam," I told him. "Check back with me in half an hour or so. That okay?"

He hooted eagerly while I returned to the inn and claimed the computer behind the desk. Then I copied my design for the leaflet from my notebook into the designing software we'd installed.

Mercy peered over my shoulder at the screen. "You're working on the assumption that this won't be over by tomorrow, then?"

"It's easier that way," I replied. "Even if it does stop, there'll be a backlog of undelivered mail from today, so this will stop people complaining about delays if they know there's a good reason."

Some of them, at any rate. I finished up my design before printing a stack of leaflets and arranging them on the desk. When I had them ready, I beckoned Sunbeam over.

"Can you distribute these around town?" I asked him. "Leave them in all the public places where people are likely to pick them up. Start with the markets and that kind of thing. Maybe ask some of the other owls to help out, but avoid drawing Dennis's attention if you can help it. Can you do that?"

He nodded enthusiastically and picked up a stack of leaflets, bound with a rubber band, in his little claws. I gave him the instructions again to make sure they'd sunk in and then waved him off. Sunbeam took flight through the open door, while I updated Mercy on our visit to Janice.

"Weird," she commented. "Either that fairy is guilty of something herself, or Janice terrorised her."

"She's still staying at her inn, though. I don't know that she'd do that if Janice was the reason she was so scared." Something definitely didn't add up. "I need to get her alone, though she moves so fast with those wings that it'll be tricky."

"Speaking of guests, I asked Kaitlyn to prepare your family's rooms on the first floor."

I slammed a palm to my forehead. "Argh. I forgot."

"Don't worry, Kaitlyn's ready."

I certainly wasn't. Let's face it, I was nowhere near prepared for the level of madness about to be unleashed upon the inn when my parents showed up. *They* weren't prepared for packages randomly falling out of the sky, but the odds of getting rid of the problem altogether before they arrived had shrunk to almost zero. As for introducing them to Spencer? I'd need to save him from the boss first.

I spent the rest of the evening doing last-minute preparations for my parents' arrival while we waited for the carollers to show up for their rehearsal. Sunbeam darted in and out between deliveries, and by the early evening, he'd sent leaflets all over town, informing the public of the disruption to the postal services. He was certainly good at his job, and if not for Dennis's personality problems, I might have suggested giving the little owl that kind of work permanently if he didn't grow big enough to deliver proper packages.

I didn't hear back from Spencer again, though for all I knew, Dennis would make him keep delivering packages all night. Instead, Mercy and I watched the carollers sing "Hark the Herald Angels Sing" repeatedly on the stage. Several of them were losing their voices, and I had the sinking suspicion that whatever flu had hit the theatre group might have already sneaked into their ranks. Mercy's mood brightened considerably when Daryl showed up for dinner with Mercy at the inn's restaurant, though I had to either play third wheel or sit with Gerry. Since he was juggling spoons in the corner, I declined his offer to act as his assistant for the night.

"Spencer's not here?" Daryl asked me sympathetically.

I shook my head. "I think he probably got tied up at work, but he hasn't messaged me in a while. I hope everything's all right."

"Maybe his boss confiscated his phone," said Mercy. "Or the battery ran out."

"Might have." I looked at the door, wondering if I should walk up to the post office and check. It was dark outside, though, and if he was still at work, Dennis wouldn't thank me for showing up again. I'd wait until morning instead. "How're rehearsals going?"

"Good," said Daryl. "Considering we had to swap the cast around. We're having issues with deliveries, though… some last-minute costumes never showed up."

My heart dropped. *Oh, no.*

"That's happening everywhere," I explained. "The post office is trying to keep up, but there's a limit to what they can do. If you open each parcel right away, it stops them from vanishing, so make sure you do that next time."

"Oh, I saw the leaflets," he said. "Did you design them yourself?"

"Yeah… how did you know?"

Mercy poked me. "I told you, you have a recognisable style. You should do this kind of thing more often."

"I do?" Creative magic might be my gift, but I'd never considered that my own style might be as distinctive as my parents'. Not in the same way, at least. I was glad that I'd been able to use my gifts in a useful way, even if I hadn't found the actual cause of the problem. If this madness didn't stop before my parents arrived, we'd be up for a second Christmas in a row of unconventional chaos… unless a miracle happened.

My thoughts went to the wishing box again, and the urge hit me to write down a wish and solve all our problems in one sweep of an owl's wings. But if the spell was the result of a wish itself, there was no telling what would result when two wishes collided.

No. There's still time to solve this without the need to make a wish. I'll make sure of it.

———

The following morning, I woke up to the sound of wings outside. Or possibly a broomstick. My parents weren't here already, were they? *Should have seen that one coming.*

After dressing as quickly as possible, I went downstairs. Another thump greeted me, and when I reached the front door, I found my view of the path outside the inn was blocked with stacked cardboard boxes.

"Those aren't ours," I murmured. "Oh, no."

I hurried upstairs to grab my phone and called Spencer, but it went straight to voicemail. As I ran for the stairs again, Mercy emerged from her room.

"What in the world is going on?" she called after me.

"Our delayed packages showed up... or someone's did, anyway."

"Oh, no." She ducked back into her room to get dressed while I left Spencer a message and went back downstairs to check on the damage.

I could barely get the front door open, and when I did, I counted at least a dozen packages sitting out on the porch. I hadn't a hope of moving them all myself, even with Mercy's help, but since I hadn't heard from Spencer yet, I didn't have much choice in the matter.

Mercy came out to join me. "What in the world are we supposed to do with these?"

I pulled out my phone. "I'll have to call the post office... but they'd need a whole fleet of reindeer to move this lot."

"Some of them might actually be ours," said Mercy. "Unlikely, though. Why'd they land here?"

"I don't know, but Spencer still isn't answering his phone."

"Maybe he crashed out as soon as he got home from delivering packages."

"Maybe." Still, worry fluttered in my chest, and I decided to stop by his place of work as soon as possible. I would prefer to see him before my parents arrived, and he might be too busy to come to the inn himself. "We'd better move these before my family shows up."

Mercy and I got to work moving the boxes aside so any potential guests would have a clear path to the door. Sunbeam must have flown out at some point in the night, because he wasn't anywhere to be found.

"Why did everything land here?" I asked nobody in particular. "We didn't order that many packages."

"Haven't a clue," said Mercy. "Unless this is Janice's work as well."

"I doubt it." Janice's message would be more explicit if it was her, and she was supposed to be preparing to kick off her event tomorrow besides. When the path to the door was clear, I checked my messages yet again and found nothing from Spencer.

"I'm going to the post office," I told Mercy. "To see if Spencer's in. He might not be, but someone needs to get these packages picked up, and I'd rather report them to Spencer than talk to Dennis on the phone."

"Good idea." She surveyed the boxes stacked at the side of the door. "I'd better tell the staff what's going on."

I set off at a fast walk, not pausing until I reached the post office. My steps came to an abrupt halt when Dennis emerged through the front door, dressed in the same green-and-gold ensemble as before. His eyes narrowed when he saw me. "What are you doing here?"

"Looking for Spencer," I said. "He's not answering his phone. Is he here?"

"No, he isn't," he said. "He checked out at midnight when his shift finished. He should be here by now, and if he's run off, I'll make him sorry."

Where was he? "He wouldn't skip work, especially at a time like this."

"So *you* say. Now, go away."

I didn't move. "We've had a dozen packages that aren't ours show up in the night. I would like to ask someone to come and fetch them."

"Get in line," he growled. "Call the office and report them that way, same as everyone else."

That was nice of him. There was no arguing when he was in this mood, though, and Spencer clearly wasn't here. As I turned away, a hooting noise sounded, and Sunbeam came flitting over to land on my shoulder.

"Is he around?" I asked Sunbeam. "Spencer, I mean? Can you see him?"

The owl shook his fluffy head, and my heart swooped downward. If he didn't know where Spencer was and neither did the boss, where had he disappeared to? There might be an innocent explanation… or our wayward spell might be claiming more than simple packages this time around.

9

I knew Spencer's address, so I resolved to stop by there on my way back to the inn. With Sunbeam sitting on my shoulder, I walked down the snowy streets until I came to his pleasant-sized cottage. The curtains were drawn, so I rapped on the door. Hard.

No reply. Sunbeam tapped on the window and hooted, then circled the house and did the same to the other windows as well, including those upstairs. Nothing. Spencer wasn't home.

"Where is he?"

Sunbeam gave a single sad hoot, while I wrenched my gaze away from Spencer's house and turned back to the inn. It was either that or hang around the post office, waiting for him to come back, and Dennis would lose his temper if he saw me there again.

He can't have just vanished. There must be an explanation. He might be so deeply asleep he hadn't heard the door, but you'd think Sunbeam's loud hooting would have woken him up. The owl perched sadly on my shoulder while I rounded the corner to the inn, crossing my fingers behind my back that we'd get the packages taken care of before any unexpected guests showed up...

Too late. My parents were already here, standing outside the inn and waiting expectantly.

Like me, my mother and father were both short and blond, but their towering hats made them look much taller than I was. Mum's hat glittered with fairy lights, while Dad's resembled a giant icicle wreathed in tinsel. Charlie, Mum's jet-black cat, sat at her feet, wearing a pointed green hat of his own, and I counted at least five suitcases between them.

My sister, Bella, lurked near the doors, wearing her usual long-suffering expression and her plain beige coat. "There you are."

My parents both gave delighted grins at the sight of me.

"It's so good to see you!" Mum wrapped me in a hug, her hat bobbing, and then Dad did the same. I ushered them inside, having to step out of the way of the suitcases and boxes as I did so.

"Sorry about the mess out here," I said to them. "You'd better come in."

Mercy came hurrying out the hall as they entered. "Sorry—I'll get Kaitlyn to carry your bags upstairs."

"You've hired more staff!" Mum remarked.

"Yes, I told you, remember?" I ducked as Sunbeam flew across to the desk to avoid crashing into Mum's hat. "Kaitlyn will sort you out. You can unpack and settle in."

The odds of them staying put were low, but Mercy's wide eyes told me that something else had happened since I'd left, while Spencer's absence left my thoughts in disarray. I gave Mercy an apologetic look, though we'd both expected my family to show up early, and she ducked into the back room with her phone clenched tightly in her hand.

Charlie the cat watched Sunbeam with interest for a moment before following the others upstairs. I hoped he wouldn't try to attack the small, fluffy owl, or else I wouldn't be able to let Sunbeam out of my sight for the duration of Spencer's absence.

Why did my family always have the worst sense of timing? Or should that be, why did the rest of the universe have the worst sense of timing? Let's face it, I'd brought this on myself by agreeing to let them come early, but I'd hardly expected Spencer to go *missing*.

Instead of following our parents upstairs, Bella eyed me. "What's going on here?"

Where to start? "We're dealing with an... incident. Starting with the fact that the post office is screwed up, which is why we have a mountain of packages outside."

"Fun," she said. "That's got to be inconvenient. Wait, doesn't your boyfriend work as a delivery guy?"

"Exactly," I said. "You should go upstairs and help Mum and Dad unpack."

"They don't need my help." She remained in front of the desk. "You clearly do."

I glanced in Mercy's direction, but she remained in the back room, talking to someone on the phone in a hushed voice. "Unless you're volunteering to deliver all those packages to their individual recipients and make sure they're opened before they disappear again, there's nothing you can do."

"I doubt it," she said. "Go on, tell me."

95

"I don't want to bring you into our drama. Or our parents, come to that."

"Why not? It worked last time."

True. I'd learned early on not to confide in my parents if I wanted things to stay on the right side of chaotic rather than spiralling out of my control… but it would be all but impossible to hide the direness of our position if my family saw the fallout up close. Besides, I ought to know from their last visit that my parents' brand of chaos might be exactly what we needed in a time of crisis.

"Fine," I relented. "I'm pretty sure Spencer is missing."

"Missing?" She raised a brow. "Did he get buried alive in packages?"

"Hilarious." I drew in a breath. "He isn't answering his phone, and he isn't at home. Or at work. He checked out at midnight, and that's the last time anyone saw him."

"Maybe he's out on a delivery," she said. "If it's true and packages are disappearing and reappearing all over the place, it's got to be hard to keep track."

"He hasn't checked in at work, though."

"He might have forgotten. Or got lost on the way to a delivery. Maybe someone got confused and put the South Pole on their address instead of the North Pole."

"Not helping, Bella," I said. "His boss thinks he's run off, and he won't help me find him. He has to deal with the fallout of a hundred-odd packages vanishing and reappearing in random locations already, so he brushed me off when I went to tell him about Spencer."

"Wouldn't finding his missing employee be in his best interests too?"

"You'd think, but his supervisor isn't acting rationally at the moment. He's under a ton of stress."

A muffled squeaking noise interrupted. Sunbeam came zipping past the desk, pursued by Charlie the cat. Somehow Mum's familiar had slipped downstairs without my noticing and had immediately targeted the owl. Oh, no.

"What is that?" Bella asked. "Is it an owl or a fluffy tennis ball?"

"Bella, you *met* Sunbeam at the Summer Solstice event, remember?" I caught the little owl before Charlie could grab him. "He works with Spencer, usually. Charlie, leave him alone."

"Oh, him," she said. "I thought they generally hired owls that could deliver things heavier than a paperclip."

Sunbeam gave an indignant hoot, while Charlie leapt onto the reception counter in an effort to grab him.

"Hey!" I shouted. "Mum, can you please get your familiar under control?"

Footsteps came from the stairs, and their owners followed. Mum and Dad entered the reception area again, hats bobbing, just as the owl broke free of my hand and flew away, narrowly missing being snagged in Charlie's claws.

"Mum, can you help me stop your familiar from eating one of the post office's owls?" I asked. "Sunbeam—no!"

The little owl bounced into the front doors, which swung open, and then flew out into the mass of packages outside. There, I belatedly noticed that several other owls had landed nearby, large eyes blinking at the inn.

"Please tell me you came to pick those up." I indicated the packages. "Ah—have you seen Spencer? Any of you?"

The owls shook their heads, economically picking up the packages in their claws. As the owls began to take flight, I noticed someone had also left a stack of leaflets in front of the doors. Specifically, *my* leaflets.

"Hey... those are mine." I ran over to the leaflets and picked them up. Had someone intentionally collected them all to drop on my doorstep? Someone like a certain angry supervisor, for instance? I'd have to tell Mercy later, because when I got back into the reception, I found Bella telling our parents about the chaos at the post office and about Spencer's subsequent disappearance. At this point, I was resigned to them finding out, though Charlie's fixation on Sunbeam was more of a pressing concern.

"Please keep him under control," I said to Mum. "Sunbeam belongs to the post office. In other words, the only people who stand a chance of helping me find Spencer. They won't help if your familiar eats one of their owls."

Mum crouched beside her familiar and lifted a struggling Charlie in her arms. "Charlie, leave the poor thing alone. When did you last hear from Spencer, Carol?"

"At some point yesterday evening," I replied. "He told me he'd drop by today, but he never showed up at work and wasn't at his house either."

"It hasn't been that long, though," Bella pointed out. "He's probably fine. As for that boss of his, I'd like to talk to him myself."

"I really wouldn't," I said. "He's been dealing with complaints for the past day, so he has an even shorter fuse than usual."

"Who is he?" asked Dad.

"The supervisor at the local post office," I said. "All the complaint calls end up going directly to him, which is unfortunate given that he has the diplomatic skills of a rampaging ape."

Bella snorted, while Mum frowned at me. "So people are getting the wrong packages? Everyone?"

"No... not at first," I explained. "Basically, if people don't open their parcels fast enough, they vanish, and they end up with someone else's instead. I'm not sure what caused it, but it's either a prank or attempted sabotage from someone who doesn't want anyone to have a nice holiday."

"And now they've kidnapped your boyfriend?"

"It's not funny, Bella."

"Never said it was," she said. "I told you, though, he probably got tied up delivering something."

"He checked out of the office, though. He's not the type to run off in the middle of a job either."

"Then we'll find out." Bella strode towards the door.

"Hang on." I shot an alarmed look at my parents, but they made no move to stop my younger sister. "Do you even know the way to the post office?"

"I can find out. Bet those owls will lead the way."

I groaned when Charlie leapt from Mum's arms and followed Bella outside, causing the post owls to scatter in alarm and drop leaflets everywhere. Mum and Dad hastened to restrain the cat and prevent him from chasing the owls—including poor Sunbeam—while I ran after my sister.

"Bella," I hissed. "Please stop. You have no idea what you're doing."

"Sure I do. I'm going to find your missing boyfriend."

"You don't even know who might be responsible." I strode after her, while my parents followed, Mum holding Charlie in her arms. "Guys, seriously. I'm not kidding when I say the boss is not to be messed with."

ELLE ADAMS

"Then he ought to be glad of our help," said Mum decisively. "Let's go."

I might as well have tried to argue with a snowman, so I hurried to keep pace as they steamrollered ahead.

"Hang on." I overtook them as we neared the post office, figuring that Dennis would be slightly less annoyed to see me walk in than a couple of strangers in outrageous hats. Not that that was saying much. "Let me ask the other employees if they've seen him before talking to the boss."

Inside the main office, the usual crowd of employees stood at the desks, sorting packages and envelopes into piles. The room appeared twice as crowded as yesterday, and I was hardly able to take a step without knocking into a box or a table.

"Back again?" Travis's voice came from behind a towering stack of envelopes. He must have seen me here last time, unless he was referring to my multiple visits to the office yesterday.

"Yes, I am," I replied. "I'm looking for Spencer. When did you last see him?"

"Yesterday morning," he answered. "Is he hiding from his responsibilities again?"

You're one to talk. "No, he's disappeared. He isn't at home and isn't answering his phone."

He made a derisive noise. "So? Maybe he doesn't want to talk to you."

Anger flared inside me, but my mother elbowed her way past me before I could speak. "How dare you say that to my daughter!"

Heat crept up my neck, while Travis peered out at her from behind his stack of envelopes. "What... who are you?"

100

"I'm Carol's mother," she informed him. "Here to help her find Spencer. Who are you, exactly?"

One of the office doors at the back slammed open, and a familiar voice rang out. "What is going on in here? Travis, are you slacking off again?"

Oh, no. A certain elf was back, and when he saw my parents, Dennis's eyes practically fell out of his skull. I didn't even blame him. There were no adequate words to sum up the bewilderment of one's first sighting of my parents and their towering hats. Not to mention Charlie the cat, who'd escaped Mum's grip and was pawing eagerly at an unopened envelope.

"We're looking for Spencer," Dad told Dennis. "You must be the boss. I'm Carol's father."

Dennis looked more baffled than angry. "Why are you in my office? You aren't employees."

"Because this was the last place Spencer was seen." Mum picked up Charlie before he could eat someone's Christmas card. "And we have to start somewhere. Don't you want to find your missing employee?"

"If he's run off in the middle of the job, then certainly not." Some of the shock disappeared from his voice, to be replaced with anger. "You aren't supposed to be in here."

"He hasn't run off," I said, despite the warning voice in my mind telling me to back off. "I went to his house, and he wasn't in. His phone number goes straight to voicemail. I think something might have happened to him."

"You're in the wrong place," Travis piped up. "All of you. Get out."

"Travis," Dennis snapped. "Get on with your job. I'll speak to these three in my office."

I blinked in surprise at him inviting us into his own

office instead of throwing us out himself. Maybe he was willing to listen... or maybe he just didn't want his staff distracted by my parents' ridiculous hats.

Whatever the case, this might be my only chance to get Spencer back. I couldn't screw it up.

Mum, Dad, Bella, and I crowded into Dennis's office, along with Charlie the cat. The office itself was the size of a cupboard but otherwise had no clutter, unlike the main office. No stray envelopes or boxes littered the floor, and I cringed when Mum's hat caught on the doorframe and started singing "Silent Night."

The boss glowered at her. "Can you shut that up?"

"Oh, of course!" Mum fiddled with the hat and accidentally turned the volume up, while I shrivelled on the spot in acute embarrassment. If I'd had a wishing box with me, I'd have wished to fall through the floor, or possibly vanish to wherever Spencer had gone. Anything other than staying in the same room as a furious elf while my parents assailed him with their ridiculous hats.

Finally, the singing halted, leaving an uncomfortable silence behind.

"Why exactly are you here?" Dennis demanded of my parents. "You'd better have a good explanation."

"Spencer is missing," I blurted. "He's not at his house and doesn't seem to be anywhere else in town either."

"I told you I don't know where he is, didn't I?" he said. "Bringing these *people* with you isn't going to change my mind."

My face heated up, but Bella stepped in. "I'd have thought it'd be in your interests to find him, considering he was helping you out with your deliveries."

"You're not from here, are you?" he growled. "I don't have time to send out a rescue mission."

"What makes you think he needs rescuing?" Bella said. I nudged her from behind pointedly, but she ignored me. "Well?"

"It's a figure of speech," Dennis growled. "Until he checks into the office, I'm assuming he's skipping work and proceeding accordingly. The last thing I need is an employee to run off and his girlfriend's family to show up and start hassling me."

He can't be behind this, can he? I'd only briefly considered the possibility, but if there'd been a wishing box in this tiny room, it wouldn't be hard to spot. The office had all the personality of a broom cupboard, and a glittering box would stand out.

"We don't mean any trouble," Dad told him. "In fact, we'd be delighted to look for Spencer ourselves. All we need to know is where he was last seen."

Dennis gave him a withering look. "If you want me to tell you the address of every client he visited in the past day, I can't do that. Not least because every package needed to be delivered twice or more."

"I understand that," I ventured, "but I don't think he

disappeared while out on a delivery. I'm not sure he even made it home."

He scowled. "Wherever he is, everyone else needs to pick up the slack, and ensuring the work gets done is more useful than debating his location."

I'd figured he'd say that, but I wasn't about to give up that easily. "Is he definitely the only person who didn't show up at work today?"

"That I know of, yes. Are you going to stop wasting my time now?"

"Just checking," I said. "Has it occurred to you that another employee might be responsible for him being absent? Like Travis, for example?"

"Don't be absurd." He glared up at me. "You're trying my patience."

"She was perfectly polite," Mum reprimanded him. "I don't like your attitude."

The expression on Dennis's face could have frozen a desert. For a moment he just goggled at her as if he hadn't a clue what to say, while Dad spoke next. "Yes, she was. You should be ashamed of yourself."

Dennis went as red as a traffic light, which seemed oddly fitting alongside his green-and-gold clothes. "You *dare* speak to me like that?"

So much for diplomacy. While I had zero desire to tick him off even more, this was my last shot at answers, and so I pulled out one of the leaflets from my pocket. "Who was responsible for dropping half the mail outside my inn as well as all these leaflets?"

"I knew those were your work." He advanced on me, wearing a menacing look on his face. "Get out. All of you. Now."

I got the message. Pushing open the door, I grabbed both my parents by the elbows in an attempt to drag them after me. Neither of them budged an inch until Bella stepped in to help me—to my surprise, given that she'd been the one who'd dragged them here to begin with—and we managed to wrangle them out of the office door. Naturally, Mum's hat started singing again in the process.

"Get out!" Dennis roared, loudly enough to make every employee in the vicinity jump a foot in the air.

This time even my parents saw the danger. All of us, including Charlie the cat, ran for the front door and out into the snow. We didn't stop until we reached the end of the road.

Bella spoke first. "That guy is in charge? Really?"

"He should be concerned for his missing employee!" Mum fumed.

"What a terrible attitude," Dad agreed.

"You're right, but we aren't going to get anywhere if we keep arguing with him," I said. "He doesn't know where Spencer is, not if he was telling the truth about him not checking in at the office since he went home last night. We're more likely to learn from someone who's actually seen him recently."

Whoever *that* was. Right now, Travis still sat at the top of my list of suspects, but what had he done to make Spencer disappear, and how could I get him back?

"You mean the employees?" Bella turned towards the office.

"We're not going back in there," I said flatly. "Please don't interrogate anyone. We need proof first."

"A spell made him vanish, do you think?" Mum asked.

"I don't know," I admitted, "but there's definitely a spell causing the packages to go to the wrong places, and it wouldn't surprise me if his disappearance had the same cause."

"A spell," said Dad. "What kind of spell?"

"I don't know yet." The wishing box hovered in my mind's eye, but it'd take a specific wish to make someone disappear, more so than the chaos with the packages.

Which all but proved this was Travis's doing, unless Janice had lost her temper yesterday after our second visit. *We were trying to help her, though.*

We made our way back towards the inn, while my parents tossed theories back and forth and Bella mostly stayed quiet. Thinking. So did I. Yet I couldn't make the clues add up. Spencer did seem to be the only staff member who'd vanished, so either his disappearance was unrelated or the person responsible had something against him *and* Holiday Haven's postal service itself. Janice was certainly petty and irrational enough to retaliate against both of us for doing her a favour, but why would she ruin the holidays for everyone else? No, it didn't add up.

Bella turned to me when we neared the inn. "You think another co-worker is behind this, don't you?"

"Unless they wanted to make their own lives more difficult, I can't think why they would," I said. "This has caused complete chaos. I'm not sure the effects are even within the control of the person who did it, and I also have no idea who the intended target was to begin with. Before Spencer vanished, I mean."

At least all the packages outside the inn had gone

away, hopefully to their intended destinations. Inside, Sunbeam the owl greeted us at the door and then flew behind the Christmas tree when Charlie approached him. The cat then reached out a paw to bat at the lower branches of the tree, causing the baubles to jangle.

"Enough," Mum reprimanded her familiar. "Leave that poor little owl alone. He's been through enough."

"He definitely has," I agreed. "Where'd Mercy go?"

"Here," came a muffled voice from behind the back door. "I'll be out in a minute."

What's going on? She'd been on the phone when I'd left, but if something had gone sideways with the event preparation, I figured she'd want to talk to me alone rather than in front of my family members.

"Mercy, did all the post owls leave?" I asked through the closed door.

"For now, but they still need to bring back the actual deliveries from yesterday."

"You mean the dozen pairs of socks I ordered." Oops. "No wonder Dennis yelled at me."

"He yelled at you?"

"It wasn't... unprovoked." I cast a glance at my blissfully unaware parents, who were currently admiring the banner above the door to the main hall. "Mum, Dad, do you want to finish unpacking? Mercy and I need to talk about the event."

"When is the event again?" asked Mum.

"It was going to start on Saturday, but we're still figuring it out. I didn't really expect Spencer to vanish."

"Then we'll find him," Dad decided. "This is a small town, right? There's only so many places he might be."

"I guess." Unless he'd vanished as the result of a spell. Then, all bets were off.

"We know our way around," Mum added. "From the last time. Remember?"

"I know," I said. "But... I mean, short of knocking on everyone's doors, I don't know how we can ask everyone if they saw him. It's pretty clear the postal staff weren't paying any attention, and who can blame them?"

"We were already going to go to the market, so we can ask around," said Dad. "We'll drop into the coffee shop to ask everyone there."

"I don't think that'll work. He's not been anywhere all week except to deliver to people's houses." My mind recoiled in horror from the notion of my parents walking around the market, asking everyone if they'd seen Spencer.

"Better than nothing," said Bella. "What were those leaflets you showed the grumpy leprechaun, anyway?"

I dug the leaflets out of my pocket and dropped them on the desk. "Warnings to the public of disruption to the post service. I made them myself, and Dennis must have taken offence at me for trying to be helpful."

"You designed these?" Mum swooped down and picked up a stack of leaflets. "Good, we'll take them with us too."

I knew a losing battle when I saw one. "I'm not sure Dennis wants the entire town to know his employee is missing. Besides, I doubt the average person knows the difference between one delivery guy and the next. They just want their mail. Preferably before Christmas."

"Then we'll find another way to get their attention."

Dad's expression brightened. "We do still have the order forms for our hats. I'll go and get them."

He ran upstairs, Mum on his tail, while I rolled my eyes at Bella. "They want to get people to order hats from them at the market?"

"As far as plans go, it's not a terrible one," said Bella. "Didn't you want to stop that Janice from dragging all the attention away from you? This ought to do the trick."

"That was before my boyfriend went missing," I pointed out. "Now can you please stop our parents from getting out of control, while I talk to Mercy?"

"All right." She rolled her eyes but did as I said and followed them upstairs. When I heard the door close, I seized the chance to duck into the hall.

"Sorry about that." I spied Mercy sitting at the edge of the stage, staring into space. "What is it? Did something else happen?"

"Most of the carollers have all come down with flu as well, including Larry," she said. "And so have three members of the main cast."

"Not Daryl?"

She inclined her head.

"Oh no." I went over and sat next to her. "What are we going to do?"

"I don't know." She sniffed. "Daryl was pretty much delirious when I spoke to him on the phone. I don't see him being in a fit state to direct everyone, and I can only hope we didn't catch the flu from him yesterday as well."

I hope not. That was all we needed. "Well... are there enough people left to perform the play?"

"Barely," she said in a small voice. "And we'll have to skip the carols in the interlude, I think. You've seen how the carollers can't function without Larry coordinating them."

"It's not the end of the world," I reassured her. "My parents were already planning on selling hats during the interlude, and if they wear their singing hats while they're there, I can guarantee most people won't notice the difference. They'll still get to listen to carols, right?"

"I guess." She lowered her head into her hands. "I don't know what we're going to do about the play, though. Daryl claimed that the others know the whole thing by heart and can rehearse without him, but he was also having trouble pulling his socks on at the time."

"They're far more resourceful than the carollers are, though." I heard footsteps in the reception area. "Hang on. I should check on my parents before they run out and start grabbing people to question about my boyfriend's whereabouts."

I left the hall at a quick stride, but it was only Gerry, who gave me a vague smile when he spotted me.

"Anything I can help you with?" I asked.

"No, but I heard the noise and wondered if you needed a hand. I saw you had a great number of parcels outside… perhaps I could move them for you?"

"It's been taken care of." If his track record was anything to go by, he might make the parcels genuinely disappear and not merely be transported across town. An idea popped into my head. "I had a question for you, though. Can a person vanish? Like your spoons?"

"Vanish?" he echoed. "A person vanished, did they? Anyone you know?"

"I don't know that that's what happened," I clarified. "I just wondered if it was possible."

"Anything is possible."

Well, that was illuminating. It probably wasn't worth twisting my brain in knots over Gerry's cryptic statements, but I also should have known better than to expect a straight answer from him.

Footsteps sounded on the stairs. My parents came ambling into view, so I dropped the subject. Gerry eyed their towering hats with his usual mildly distracted expression and overlooked Bella altogether.

"Gerry—this is my family," I told him. "My mum and dad... and that's my sister, Bella, at the back. Mum, Dad, this is Gerry. He's our only other guest at the inn right now."

"It's great to meet you!" Mum beamed at him, while Dad leapt in to shake his hand, hat bobbing. None of it seemed to faze Gerry in the slightest, and after greeting them, he sauntered off upstairs.

When he'd disappeared from sight, Mum scooped up the remaining leaflets from the counter to distribute around the market.

"You really don't have to," I protested. "Dennis will probably have his owls drop them back at the inn like he did before."

"Then he's a fool," said Dad. "The public has to know about the disruption to the postal service, don't they?"

"That was the intention, but I really don't want to annoy Dennis even more than I already have." Granted, he'd already proven he couldn't help me find Spencer— and it was hard to worry about him being forced to work on Christmas Day when he might not return at all. I pushed that thought out of mind and asked, "Are you actually going to sell hats at the market?"

"We haven't sorted out our stock yet, so we'll just be taking orders," said Mum. "We'll ask for anyone interested in buying a hat to fill out the order form and come to collect their orders at the inn. That way they'll be directly exposed to your event. What do you think?"

"Not a bad plan." I glanced at the door to the main hall, from which Mercy had yet to emerge. "We're trying to revamp our schedule, though. The carollers have come down with flu, and so has the leader of the theatre group. So we're going to have to come up with something else for the intermission."

"Seriously?" Bella's brows rose. "Bad timing."

"Tell me about it," I said. "Mum, Dad, are you okay with using your singing hats as a replacement for the carollers at the interlude of the play?"

"Of course!" said Dad. "We can even make more."

"I'm sure the ones you have will be enough," I told him. "As for the play… we'll see how it works out, but if you wow them with their hats, it might not matter if everything else is a bit haphazard."

"Then we'll do our best!" Mum said. "Come on, let's go, Charlie."

Her cat, who'd been poking at the tree where Sunbeam was hiding, followed my parents out of the door. Bella, meanwhile, remained behind.

"I shouldn't have encouraged them," I said to her. "They're going to be insufferable now."

"At least they'll be out of trouble," said Bella.

"Out of trouble?" I echoed. "Not likely. They're certain to make a spectacle at the market."

"Isn't that what you want?" she asked. "They'll draw people to the inn and spread word about Spencer's disappearance at the same time. It might even stop that Dennis from mistreating his employees."

"Not sure about that," I said. "I don't like him, and neither does Spencer, but he's dealing with an impossible situation at the moment."

"Unless he's the one behind this," she added. "Have you thought of that one?"

"I've already dismissed that theory. Come on, would the guy in charge of the postal service want to screw everything up?"

"It's as good a guess as any." She gave a shrug. "Who else could it possibly be?"

"Travis. But Dennis won't let us go into the post office to question him again, and I've already tried and failed to get him to admit to anything."

"You know, there's an easy way to fix this without any complications." Bella's voice dropped in volume. "Why not get that wishing box out again?"

"Nope," I said flatly. "It's going to be part of our event like last year, but Mercy and I vowed not to use it for anything other than minor things like asking for presents."

"Not even when it might solve all our problems?"

"It might have *caused* all our problems."

I hadn't intended to let that slip, but Bella's eyes rounded in response. "What? Someone got the box out again?"

"Not our wishing box," I clarified, hoping Mercy couldn't hear us. "There's a chance this chaos might be the result of an out-of-control wish, but there's no proof to back it up yet."

If I mentioned Janice's mysterious guest, I knew Bella

would be on her doorstep in a heartbeat, but if this had been a fairy-induced wish, it would have run out at midnight. Besides, I'd prefer to have exhausted all other possible options before we did anything drastic like ticking off my main rival.

From Bella's expression, though, she wasn't about to let this one drop easily.

11

While Bella watched me with a pensive look on her face, Sunbeam flew out from behind the tree and landed on the desk.

Bella glanced at the little owl. "Did he see Spencer before he left?"

"I honestly don't know. I found him at the post office." Pity Sunbeam couldn't speak, really, but if he hadn't followed Spencer when he'd left the office, he might not know where he'd gone afterwards.

A calculating expression crossed her face. "Does he know the addresses of all the staff too? Including the ones who might be hiding something they shouldn't have?"

"Bella, we're not breaking into anyone's houses."

"We don't have to." She indicated Sunbeam. "He's small enough to slip through a window, isn't he?"

"Whose window?" I frowned. "You mean Travis's."

If he had a wishing box, then he wouldn't be foolish enough to carry it around with him. He'd have hidden it at home. But we'd be taking a major risk if he didn't turn out to have one at all. Or if he'd used someone else's.

"It's that or snoop around the post office and hope the angry leprechaun doesn't ambush us again." Bella shrugged. "I'm good with either."

I had no other ideas at hand, so I addressed the owl. "Sunbeam, do you want to go to the post office and look for Spencer?" I'd broach the subject of a potential break-in later.

He nodded enthusiastically, so I went into the hall first to check with Mercy. I didn't want to leave her alone, but there was nothing we could do to fix the event until we'd heard from the rest of the theatre group about whether they could continue with the show without Daryl.

Mercy glanced up at me with bloodshot eyes. "You're going out?"

"Bella and I are going to snoop around, if that's okay. Also, Mum and Dad are handling signups to buy hats at the market, and their customers will have to come here to collect them. That ought to get us plenty of publicity for the event."

"Just how many hats are they planning on making this weekend?"

"I think they already brought them." I gave her a concerned look. "Will you be okay here alone? Or do you want me to help with the event?"

"No... I'll stop moping." She rose to her feet, seeming to pull herself together. "This is normally the point where I'd ask Daryl to stop by to reassure me I'm not going to screw this up, but right now he's too delirious to tell his left foot from his right one."

"Oh, no," I said. "If you want to pay him a visit, let me

know, and I'll take over from you."

She gave a shaky smile. "I'm good. Thanks, though."

Bella gave me a questioning look when I returned to the reception area. "She's not handling the crisis well, is she?"

"No... well, Janice didn't help matters by moving up her schedule by a day, and you can't blame her for panicking that the theatre group are dropping like flies from this flu thing. Anyway, we should go."

Bella and I left the inn, and I marvelled at how much had changed in the past year. My sister and I hadn't always got along. In fact, we'd been mortal enemies for years in the way only siblings could be, but she'd matured dramatically in recent years. Now I was glad of her help, but I knew better than to think Dennis would be willing to talk to us again even without our parents being present.

Once again, Sunbeam led the way to the post office, but I brought Bella to a halt before we reached the doors.

"There's a way around the side where we can see into the office without anyone spotting us... if we hide behind the trees, that is," I told her. "I'm not sure what we're actually looking for, though."

Bella studied the building. "You think someone in there is messing with wishing boxes?"

"Not *in* there. If a wishing box is involved at all, I don't think anyone would use it where everyone could see them. Also, Travis caught me spying on him through the window last time, so he's even more likely to take care not to do anything that would give him away."

"He's your main suspect?"

"He hates Spencer for no good reason," I explained.

"But he claimed the weirdness with the packages wasn't his work."

"So he's the one whose address you didn't want to go to," she surmised. "You know, I bet the post office has a list of recent orders. If we got hold of the right paperwork, we can find out if anyone has ordered a wishing box recently."

"There's no way they'd leave that information lying around," I said. "Besides, if an employee is responsible, they might even have messed with the records."

"Good thinking there." A gleam entered her eyes. "You can't buy one of those things from the market, can you?"

"No, but swiping the office's paperwork is riskier than breaking into Travis's house, and that's saying a lot." My gaze drifted over to Sunbeam, who'd perched on a nearby tree branch. "I suppose I can ask Sunbeam to sneak a look through the windows of his house. That's not breaking in."

"Exactly." She gave an approving nod, while I wondered just what she'd been doing in the six months since we'd last seen each other for her to have developed such a taste for detective work. "Let's go."

"Sunbeam." I beckoned to the owl. "Do you know Travis's address?"

He dipped his head and let out a low hoot before taking flight.

"Wait for us." I hastened to follow him without being seen by anyone in the post room, but he flew at a speed that surprised me.

Bella snickered under her breath. "Guess he's happy to break the law if it means getting Spencer back."

"Travis was rude to him the last time they spoke, so

I'm not surprised." Still, I hoped this wouldn't backfire on us.

Bella and I followed Sunbeam down the snowy streets until we came to a cottage similar to Spencer's own house. Nobody was in, by the looks of things, but I ducked my head and whispered to Sunbeam, "If you see a sparkly box of any sort, let me know. You know what the wishing box looks like, right?"

Sunbeam hooted an affirmative and then zipped up to look through an upper window of the house. Bella and I waited outside while he circled the house and peered through all the windows.

"Hey, that one's open." She pointed. "Can you wriggle through there?"

"So much for not breaking in."

But Sunbeam was happy to squeeze through the slightly open window, while I cringed at the thought of Travis's reaction if he returned from work to find his house in a mess.

"It's a good job he lives alone," I whispered. "I hope Sunbeam doesn't wreck the place."

Or maybe I didn't, if he was the real reason for Spencer's disappearance. Several minutes passed before Sunbeam emerged through the crack in the window and shook out his rumpled feathers.

"Anything?"

A sad hoot was the only response.

My shoulders slumped. "Did you look everywhere?"

If Travis didn't own a wishing box, then either someone else had one in their possession, or a certain fairy was involved after all.

"Weird," Bella murmured. "Anyone else you suspect

from the office?"

"No, and I'm done with breaking and entering for the day." I turned away from Travis's house, and so did Bella, to my relief.

"Interesting," she said as we walked. "If he doesn't have a wishing box, then it might be another spell at work."

"Might be." I debated for a moment then pushed ahead. "I have another idea, but no proof to back it up. I think Janice has a fairy staying at her inn… and you know the last fairy we met could grant wishes."

Bella stopped in her tracks. "You think Janice has a fairy who can grant wishes at her inn? And she did this?"

"It's a major leap to make," I told her. "I did see a fairy at her inn, yes, but there's no guarantee that she can grant wishes, much less that she's responsible for this mess. She also seemed terrified of me."

"Interesting." She pursed her lips. "Why's that, I wonder?"

"I'm guessing Janice told her lies about me, but that doesn't mean she's the bad guy," I said firmly. "If not Travis, Janice is my next suspect, but I don't understand why she's acting as if we're bitter rivals again."

"Is she now?" said Bella. "Maybe she wanted to strike first, then."

"I literally haven't spoken to her in months. It makes zero sense for her to randomly start antagonising me again."

"Didn't she get paranoid about you doing stuff to her which turned out to be someone else instead?" she asked. "Maybe it's a repeat of last year."

She had a point. "I asked what her problem was and got a nonanswer. I'm not sure that's it, though."

For one thing, she wasn't the direct target of anything that might be attributed to the wishing box. She'd been mad at me before her package had disappeared, besides.

"Even if it isn't Janice, her fairy guest might still be involved," said Bella. "If she's acting guilty already, it's worth questioning her."

"She seemed more scared than guilty." I thought back. "I do want to talk to her again, but she's likely to run off if we corner her. I don't think the direct approach is going to work, to be honest."

"She's definitely staying at Janice's inn?"

"Yeah, and I only saw her because I offered to help Spencer deliver Janice's mail... twice," I added. "Janice didn't open the package fast enough the first time around, so it disappeared again."

"Do you think Janice did it on purpose?" she asked. "To make things more difficult for you and Spencer?"

"That's a stretch too," I said. "But the last time I saw Spencer was after he made the second delivery."

"There's your excuse for paying her a visit, then." Bella changed directions, presumably remembering the way to Janice's inn from last time. "Ask her if she's seen him."

"I'm pretty sure that if I ask Janice if she kidnapped Spencer, she'll kick me out."

Her own paranoia had zero basis in reality, but mine might be equally dubious. Yet who knew, maybe her fairy guest would be able to provide a clue we sorely needed.

"Got a better idea?" said Bella.

"I think we should wait for Mum and Dad to get back first, so they can give us any leads they have," I decided. "If Janice's name comes up again, we'll have a reason to talk to her."

"We already do," she said. "Unless you want me to tell Mum and Dad that there's a wish involved."

"You wouldn't." She would, though, and it wasn't even a desire to be the annoying younger sibling that drove her this time around. For reasons I couldn't fathom, she'd positioned herself as my ally. "Bella, the very last thing we need is the entire town to know there might be a rogue wish messing with their mail."

"Come on." She walked faster. "It's worth finding out what this fairy knows."

"She's not going to agree to talk to you," I said. "Neither is Janice, since I crossed a line yesterday when I showed up twice to deliver her mail. Unless you throw a net at that fairy... don't get any ideas."

Bella grinned slyly. "Nah, we'll just ask Janice if she's seen your boyfriend."

"Because I really want *her* to know he's missing."

"If she's responsible, then she'll already know," she said. "And if it turns out her guest is sneakily granting wishes to someone else, she might even thank us for telling her."

"I doubt it." But this might be our only chance to find out if she knew where Spencer had gone before her event kicked off, and we were out of any other options.

Hoping she was in a diplomatic mood, I approached Janice's inn. First I directed Sunbeam to peek through the windows and let me know if the fairy was in her room. He dropped down a moment later and shook his head, and Bella whispered, "See if you can get in through the window."

I elbowed her in the ribs, but Sunbeam took off for the upper windowsill and began nudging it with his beak. Resigned, I left him to it and entered the inn.

Behind the desk, Janice rolled her eyes when she saw me. Then her gaze went to Bella. "I know you."

"This is my sister, Bella," I said. "She and my parents are here to visit for the holidays."

"Oh, the weirdos."

"Speak for yourself."

"Why are you here?" she asked. "Not enough room at the inn, is there? Too bad—I'm fully booked."

"That's not the problem." Did she seriously think I'd make my family members stay at *her* inn? They'd probably wake up to ants in their beds. "Did your box stay put this time around?"

"Yes, not that it's any of your business. Why?"

I drew in a breath. "Have you seen Spencer since yesterday?"

"No, I have not. Lost him, have you?"

I looked at her sharply. "Spencer hasn't been seen by anyone since he left work last night, and the last time I saw him was right here. He isn't answering his phone either."

She blinked. "You're telling me your boyfriend is missing?"

"I guess I am," I said. "Since I last saw him when we delivered your package for the second time, I figured I'd check if you'd seen him more recently."

"Oh." She tilted her head. "I see how it is. You think I'm to blame, do you?"

"No, but this was the last place I saw him." I glanced up at a faint thud from upstairs. *Sunbeam.* "I'm trying to piece together where he might have gone."

"Well, you're in the wrong place," she said. "And no, I don't have any more deliveries scheduled. *My* event is already fully prepared."

Did she know ours wasn't? "I thought the theatre group all had flu. And the carollers."

"I have my own entertainment instead." She motioned towards the door. "Now, go away."

"Are you sure about that?" Bella stepped forward, ignoring my warning look. "It's interesting that you'd jump to the conclusion that we're accusing you. Either you believe the entire universe revolves around you, or you've got something to hide."

Janice flushed. "Excuse me?"

"You heard me," said Bella. "It's one or the other, and I'd say the odds are about even."

Janice stalked out from behind the desk, arms folded. "Get *out*. This is your last warning."

A bright light flashed. I took an alarmed step back, but it was Bella's hands that were the source of the light. A bracelet gleamed on her wrist that I hadn't seen before, and its crystalline surface glowed brightly enough to dazzle the eyes.

Janice stopped in her tracks. "What is that?"

Sparks flew from the bracelet, bouncing off the walls and causing Janice to leap behind the counter with a cry of alarm.

"Bella!" I grabbed her arm. "Bella, come on. We're going."

I all but dragged her outside, letting go of her arm the instant we were on the other side of the door. A tingle like static electricity ran to my fingertips, and a shiver ran down my spine.

"Bella… what *was* that?"

Bella glared at Janice through the door. "A little trick I learned."

"Not from our parents?" Like me, she never used her magical gifts at all, but I'd certainly never seen our parents create a bracelet that could give someone an electric shock.

"No," she said. "They know I've been learning, but not what I've been doing with it."

"Please tell me you're not in the habit of threatening people." That answered the question of what my sister had been doing in my absence. "Janice is going to have it in for us now, and you just blew our chances of ever having a diplomatic—"

Sunbeam interrupted by toppling out of the upper window with a shriek. I caught him in my hand before he hit the ground, turning away from the inn.

Twitching his wings, Sunbeam coughed and spat out a wad of paper into my palm.

"Where in the world did you get this?" I picked up the paper gingerly with my other hand. "Not the fairy's room?"

He nodded and took flight again while I unfolded the paper and Bella leaned over my shoulder to read the words. Unfortunately, most of them were too smudged to make out. Two stood out at the start, though… *I wish.*

"I think this is a request to a fairy godmother," said Bella. "Or a wishing box. Probably the former."

So it's true. "Whatever it is, it's safe to say we won't be getting to chat to Janice's guests anytime soon."

Bella's calculating expression was back. "We'll see about that."

12

To my relief, I didn't need to argue with Bella to get her to leave Janice's inn behind. If the fairy had been present, it'd have been a different story, though. I could tell from her scheming face that she was thinking about ways to corner the elusive fairy.

When we neared the inn, I paused in my tracks. "Might be an idea to check on Mum and Dad at the market... *if* you can refrain from using your magic to put someone's eye out."

"Oh, come on." She scoffed. "Don't look so scandalised. It's just a few sparks, nothing more than a party trick."

"Then why do you wear it everywhere?"

She shrugged. "I don't know. Why do Mum and Dad wear their hats everywhere?"

"To advertise their business." I shook my head at her. "Their hats don't tend to attack people either."

"They *could*," she said. "Look, I had an instinct you'd got into trouble again. That's all."

I *hoped* that was all, because that kind of magic could

be downright dangerous when misapplied. Then again, the same could be said of our parents' novelty hats. "Can you please not use magic on anyone while we're outside, even if they annoy you?"

"Chill out," she said. "Janice was on the brink of forcibly throwing us out, you know. And what if she did somehow disappear your boyfriend?"

"If she did, she didn't do it alone."

"That fairy guest of hers." Her gaze travelled over the snowy rooftops. "Think she might be at the market?"

"It's a popular tourist destination." The fairy had seemed pretty shy, but that might have been a reaction to me, not people in general. "The instant she sees us, she'll fly off."

"We can grab her."

"Please don't." That would only make Janice even more inclined to retaliate against us. "Let's see if Mum and Dad found any clues before we annoy anyone else."

Bella and I headed in the direction of the market, accompanied by Sunbeam. It didn't take us long before we heard the commotion of a large crowd near the market stalls. *Oh boy.*

Mum and Dad stood in the middle of the market with microphones in their hands and broad smiles on their faces. Around them, people were passing a clipboard around and adding their names to a list.

"Wow, they're getting lots of orders," said Bella. "They must have given everyone the sales pitch."

"I doubt they remembered to ask anyone about Spencer, but that might be for the best." I certainly didn't hear my boyfriend's name among the crowd, just an endless list of exclamations and questions about magical hats. I wouldn't have had a hope of spotting the fairy in the dense crowd either, but my parents spied Bella and me at once. *Oh, no.*

Mum spoke into the microphone. "There's my daughters!"

The last part of my dignity departed as the crowd moved to let Bella and me walk through to our parents' sides. Bella wore a resigned expression, while I gritted my teeth in an approximation of a smile.

"Mum," I whispered. "Dad—have you found out anything yet? About Spencer?"

"Nothing yet," Dad whispered to me. "But everyone who signed the form will have to come and collect their hats from the inn, so we can ask them in person."

Spencer will have been missing for more than a day by then. But people kept elbowing their way to the front of the crowd to ask about hats and made it impossible to get a word in edgeways. Not to mention escape. Bella and were hemmed in by the crowd, unable to move.

Sunbeam came to the rescue. A loud hooting noise sounded, and he shot through the crowd like a feathery bullet. When everyone moved aside, I seized my chance to make an escape, grabbing Bella by the wrist on my way out. She yanked herself free of my grip when we reached the outskirts of the market.

"Wow, they're popular," she said. "I guess everyone was waiting to get more hats."

"But not find Spencer." They might end up here answering questions for hours, at this rate, which meant Bella and I were on our own. "I don't think the fairy's here, either. Let's head back to the inn and regroup."

Luckily, Bella agreed, and we left the market before

people started flagging us down to ask questions about hats as well.

Once we were back at the inn, I closed the door firmly behind me and sighed.

"What's up?" Mercy asked. "Did Janice throw you out?"

"Pretty much," I said. "Also, Mum and Dad decided to make a spectacle of us at the market."

It belatedly occurred to me that I should have given the crowd the pitch for our event, but at this rate, the hats would be the entirety of the entertainment on offer.

"I figured they would," said Bella. "Besides, I told you, we need to take the initiative. Find that fairy."

"You really think it's the fairy who's doing this?" asked Mercy. "Wasn't she at the inn?"

"No, but someone sent her a note asking for a wish," I admitted. "Sunbeam found it in her room. If she was at the market, though, I hadn't a hope of finding anyone in that crowd."

"No problem," Bella said. "We can wait back at Janice's inn and waylay her."

"Because that'll go over well."

"If she's selling wishes, then we have to know who's buying."

Unfortunately, Bella was right, but how were we supposed to ambush someone who clearly had no desire to talk to me? "What if she doesn't come back to the inn?"

"Sunbeam can find her," Bella went on.

"He doesn't know her." I looked up at the little owl, who'd perched on the Christmas tree again. "If he could find missing people, he'd have already found Spencer."

"The fairy isn't missing," Bella said. "Seriously, I know you don't want to go with the direct approach, but this fairy seems too elusive to snag any other way. And if you don't want to cross Janice again, getting hold of her outside of the inn is our only option."

She had a point. Our parents still hadn't returned from the market and probably had no intention of leaving until the public's questions had dried up. Which might take hours, considering it'd been a year since their last visit. That left Bella and me... and Sunbeam, of course.

I addressed the owl. "If you fly high enough above town, do you think you can spot the fairy we saw at Janice's inn?"

Sunbeam nodded his fluffy head.

"And drop a net on them?" Bella put in.

"Not that," I said hastily. "We just need to find her, that's all."

Sunbeam hooted in understanding before taking flight out of the inn's front doors. Bella and I waited outside, watching him soar over the rooftops.

Then the owl veered around in the air, visible as a fluffy speck growing larger as he returned to the inn. When he swooped in to land, he gave a single hoot of joy.

"You found her?" I glanced at Bella, warning her not to try anything that might alarm the fairy, and then let the owl take the lead.

We left the inn behind, following the route towards the market again. Before we reached it, we rounded a corner to see a familiar winged figure heading towards us. With a frightened squeak, she wheeled around on the spot and flew away.

"Oh, no." I broke into a panicked run, as did Bella, but the fairy was far faster than I was. I didn't have wings, after all—but Sunbeam did.

ELLE ADAMS

As the fairy fled, the owl flew headlong into her with the force of a feathery bullet, knocking both of them sideways into a snowdrift. The fairy surfaced, snow covering her wings. Up close, her pointed features put me in mind of one fairy in particular, but not the expression of utter terror when she saw us approach.

"Wait!" I skidded to a halt. "I just want to ask you a question."

"I can't." She beat her wings to flee, but the snow weighed her down, slowing her pace. "Please leave me alone."

"I know the Fairy Godmother." I couldn't think of anything else to say that might stop her from fleeing. "Is she a relation of yours?"

Confusion and surprise mingled with fear in her expression. "She's my aunt. I'm Patricia. How do you know her?"

Good. I'd guessed right. "She stayed at our inn last summer, and we became friends. You don't need to be scared of me. I don't know what Janice told you, but it isn't true."

"Exactly." Bella walked over to her, and the fairy jumped violently again. "I'm her sister. Carol won't admit it, but her boyfriend went missing, and she thinks someone wished him out of existence."

"Bella!" I exclaimed.

The fairy blinked in confusion. "Wished him out of existence?"

"We don't know where he went." Might as well lay all the cards on the table now Bella had given the game away. "He went missing after delivering that package to Janice's inn yesterday. You saw him, right?"

"Oh, right." Her brow wrinkled. "Really? He went missing because of a wish? Whose?"

"I was hoping you could tell us that," Bella interjected. "You can grant wishes, can't you? We know you're taking commissions."

"*Bella*," I reprimanded her. To Patricia, I added, "I just want to know where he is."

"I don't know." A flush spread across her pointed face. "I… I'm not supposed to tell anyone who I'm related to, but some people found out and gave me messages to take her. I can't grant wishes like she can, though. There's only one Fairy Godmother."

"Wait, you can't?" Then the paper Sunbeam had found in her room must have been intended for her aunt. "Why did Janice tell you to avoid me?"

She flushed even deeper, her wings beating faster. "You've been known to make wishes before."

"I already have a wishing box," I told her. "Not that I actually use it, because it was a complete disaster last year for reasons that Janice probably remembers. Did she tell you that I was going to pounce on your aunt and make her grant my wishes?"

Patricia didn't reply, which was answer enough. I made a mental note to give the Fairy Godmother a call when we got back to the inn, assuming she didn't tell me to get lost as soon as she found out that someone in town was messing with wishes again.

"It's not true," I went on. "So the other guests are giving you their wishes?"

"Not the guests," she said. "They're performers, so they barely know I'm there. They're too busy rehearsing for the—"

"Event." So *that* was how she'd managed to move it up by a day without creating a scheduling nightmare. "Did she—?" I broke off when Bella grabbed my arm.

I twisted to look behind me, my heart sinking in my chest. Janice herself stalked towards us, and she did *not* look pleased.

"Why are you interrogating my guest?" she demanded.

"You've been telling her lies about me," I said. "You know perfectly well that the Fairy Godmother and I were friends, and I didn't force her to grant any wishes for me."

"You have a wishing box, don't you?" she said. "Use that to find your missing boyfriend, and quit hounding me. Patricia, come back to the inn."

I hoped she'd refuse, but the fairy's fear came back at the sight of Janice's evident fury. With a beat of her wings, she followed Janice, and the pair of them disappeared from sight.

"She's using her wishes," Bella said in a low voice. "Janice is. I knew it."

"The Fairy Godmother doesn't take wishes from people she hasn't met." And Patricia couldn't grant them. Unless she'd lied, but why had she ended up at Janice's inn in the first place? "No, it's not her."

"Then it's a wishing box," Bella said. "Someone in town has one, and they must have acquired it recently."

"Not Travis, unless he has another hiding place." Not Janice either. "I'm not breaking into the post office, Bella. Not even to look at their records."

"It's not breaking in if it's a public office." She grinned. "I can create a diversion so you can sneak in and take a peek at the list of recent orders."

"What *have* you been doing in the last six months?" I asked. "Watching spy movies?"

"Maybe I've been bored," she said. "Come on, I don't get nearly this much excitement at home. Not with Mum and Dad hovering around me. I see why you wanted to get away."

"I'd happily trade away our disasters, but seriously, Bella." I shook my head at her. "The post office is in chaos trying to get everything delivered in time for the holidays. The very last thing they need is you to force them out of the office with that magic of yours and then steal their paperwork."

"I can create a temporary diversion," she said. "It won't take more than a few minutes to get in and out, and I reckon their employees would be grateful for a quick break."

She wasn't wrong, but I wasn't entirely sure I trusted Bella's ability to restrain herself after what I'd seen her do at Janice's inn. "Dennis will suspect us right away. I guarantee he will."

"Not if I'm sneaky enough." Bella turned to Sunbeam. "He knows where the right paperwork is kept, doesn't he?"

Sunbeam nodded in agreement, while I groaned.

"Fine," I relented. "If we're going to do this, it'll have to be straight in and out. Nothing too complicated. And *don't* throw sparks around the office, Bella. I doubt anyone wants their Christmas shopping to be set on fire."

"I have another way," she said. "Shall we be off?"

13

Once again, Bella and I walked to the post office. I hoped she was telling the truth and that her diversion wouldn't be too outrageous. At least it didn't involve hats, but I'd almost rather it did, considering I had ample experience with magical hats and almost zero with Bella's own new branch of unexpected magic.

"Relax," she whispered to me. "Sunbeam can go in by himself, can't he? I'll take care of the distraction, and you don't have to do anything but keep watch."

I wasn't too sure about that one, but it was too late for second thoughts. If not a fairy, a wishing box must be responsible for the current madness, and since we hadn't found one in Travis's house, then it must be elsewhere in town. The quickest route to finding its location was to look into recent orders, and the post office kept track of everything.

Yet I wished I had a clearer sense of direction. We

were gambling on guesswork and nothing more, and the risks of being caught were clear enough. I ducked around the corner of the building and concealed myself behind the trees, Sunbeam perching above me.

Bella, meanwhile, approached the building with a determined stride. The window was partly open again, and I held my breath when she stood on tiptoe to push something through the gap.

An instant later, she ran behind the trees to join me, and we backed away from the building as the sound of what appeared to be a burglar alarm went off at full volume. Owls took flight in a chorus of hoots, while Dennis bellowed, "Everyone out!"

The thunder of footsteps mingled with the owls' hoots as everyone left the office at once, while Bella and I remained crouching around the corner until we were certain the elf wasn't about to come looking for intruders. We had to duck into the bushes to avoid being spotted by any of the post owls, but when the sky cleared, we had our chance.

"Sunbeam," I murmured. "Go."

The owl took flight towards the building and darted in through the open window. I kept a wary distance, but barely a minute passed before he returned, beckoning to me with his clawed foot. He wanted me to follow him.

"I can't climb through the window," I whispered. "Even if I fit, I'd get caught."

He jabbed a claw to the left-hand side, around the back of the building.

"Might be an emergency exit around there?" Bella asked. "He needs your help. Go on."

So much for this being simple. I circled the building from behind and spied a door near the back. Sunbeam zipped over to it and tapped on the wooden surface with a claw.

I pushed against the door, wincing at the noise when it opened into the main post room. Not that anyone would be able to hear it over the wailing alarm from somewhere inside the office—but it was only a matter of time before Dennis came back in to find the source. It was a wonder he hadn't already.

Sunbeam flew through the door to Dennis's office, and my throat went dry. The idea of trespassing in *there* was as appealing as diving into a snowdrift in my underwear, but where better to find the records than in the boss's office? I hurried after the little owl, who landed next to the computer on the desk. Sunbeam tapped his foot on the keyboard, bringing up a spreadsheet.

I sat down in the office chair, my heart racing. If anyone had bought a wishing box, it'd be listed somewhere, so my gaze roved up and down the page. No mention of a wishing box showed up, though I scrolled as fast as possible to read over the orders.

Sunbeam let out an urgent twittering noise. Heart lurching, I jumped out of the seat and fled the office just as the door to the post room opened.

I dropped into a crouch behind the nearest stack of parcels, thanking the universe that the room was so full of packages that there was no shortage of hiding places.

Dennis stalked into the room. "You again?"

My blood iced over—but he'd addressed Sunbeam instead of me. The owl took flight in a wild zigzag and then dove behind a desk, picking up a bracelet that resembled the one Bella had been wearing around her wrist earlier. So that was the source of the noise.

As Dennis seized the bracelet, I realised the owl had given it to him to divert his attention. Seizing my chance, I awkwardly shuffled on my knees behind the desk until I reached the back door and flung myself outside.

Then I ran as fast as possible, hoping Sunbeam didn't get into trouble for Bella's prank. If the boss found out I'd been scrolling through his records… there was no proof it was me, but Sunbeam had let himself get caught to give me the chance to escape.

Bella came running from the direction of the post office and caught up to me, eyes glittering with amusement at the chaos she'd left behind her. "Did you find what you needed?"

"I read the records, but nobody ordered a wishing box at all in the past week or two." If they'd done so at an earlier date, then I wouldn't have a chance of finding out, so I'd have to assume otherwise. "I had to leave Sunbeam in the office. He distracted the boss when he came back into the office and found that bracelet thingy you left in there."

A grin curved her mouth. "He'll have a job and a half turning that thing off."

I didn't find the situation nearly as amusing as she did. I wouldn't do us any favours by hanging around outside if Dennis happened to come in this direction looking for the culprit, so I headed back towards the inn instead.

Back in the reception area, Mercy raised her brows at us. "What did you do?"

"Broke into the post office," I told her. "Oh, and

ambushed Janice's guest. We're really doing a great job at making friends here."

"Wait, you spoke to the fairy?" she asked.

A hooting noise interrupted, to my relief. Sunbeam must have got away after all. The little owl zipped into the reception area, followed by Charlie the cat. A moment later, both my parents entered the inn.

"Did you find him?" Mum asked without preamble.

"Did I find—?" I broke off. "If you mean Spencer, no, I didn't. Instead, I'm pretty sure we just made enemies of the entire postal service as well as Janice."

Dad gave Bella a questioning look, and she shrugged. "She's exaggerating. Janice already disliked her, and the post office staff didn't know it was us who caused the disruption."

Sunbeam gave a sad hoot, and I shot my sister a look. "I'm pretty sure Sunbeam got into trouble with his boss for our sakes, and it wasn't even worth it."

"Hold on," said Mercy. "What were you even looking for at the post office?"

"Records of whether someone ordered a wishing box." Might as well get it all out in the open. "It wasn't the fairy's doing, so if this was caused by a wish, it's the only explanation I can think of."

"Wait, it's *not* the fairy?" she echoed. "How do you know?"

"She's the Fairy Godmother's niece, but she doesn't have the same abilities."

"The Fairy Godmother's niece?" Mum echoed. "The Fairy Godmother can grant wishes, can't she?"

"Yes, but her niece can't. She's been hiding from me because she thinks I'm going to pounce on her and order her to pass on my demands to her aunt when she shows up in town."

"That's what Janice told her?" Dad guessed. "Why, we should go and talk to her right now and put her right."

"I already did. Please—don't." I glanced at Mercy, who'd gone pale. "No more conflict. My next idea was to call the Fairy Godmother and ask when she's coming to town. She's more of an expert on wishes than I am."

If I'd thought, I might have called her from the start and asked if any of her relatives were around. It seemed obvious in hindsight.

"Are you sure it's a wish?" Mercy's voice was quiet. "And—wait, you really mean the Fairy Godmother is going to come to town soon?"

"According to her niece," I said. "Her name's Patricia, and I told her that her aunt and I were friends. I'm not sure she believed me, but it doesn't matter at this point. Spencer is gone, and if it was the result of a wish, then it's beyond me to figure out who did it."

Mercy picked up her phone with shaking hands. "I have the Fairy Godmother's number. I'll call her and ask her to help."

"Go ahead," I said. "She might be able to fix this. I don't think anyone else can at this point."

While Mercy backed into the room behind the desk, I faced my parents and Bella. "Until we get an answer, I'd appreciate it if nobody antagonises anyone else."

"Is there anything we can do?" asked Dad. "You definitely think a wish is doing this?"

"I'm having some doubts, given that nobody seems to have a wishing box," I said. "Unless they have a secret contact with the Fairy Godmother, but I don't see *her* consenting to screw up our postal system."

"There's another possibility," Bella put in. "Perhaps the person responsible is high enough up at the post office that they could have hidden the records. Where does that leprechaun live?"

"He's an elf, not a leprechaun, and we are *not* going after him again." I put my foot down. "I'm pretty sure he's spent the entire week in his office, and I doubt he'd have wanted to make his own life a living nightmare, either. If he finds out that spell was yours, he'll blacklist our inn for life and probably drive us all out of town."

"And that colleague of Spencer's?" Bella suggested, not to be deterred. "He's still a possible suspect, right?"

"Him or Janice." Unless Patricia had been secretly granting wishes all along, I didn't see how either of them could have convinced the Fairy Godmother to cause this level of disruption. Let alone cause Spencer to vanish.

Maybe the Fairy Godmother would be able to help. Putting our faith in wishes to solve this was a bad idea, but what else was there to do? Spencer had been missing for almost a full day now.

"Want us to talk to anyone else?" asked Mum.

"No," I said firmly. "We've exhausted our list of people we can question, and the post office is currently recovering from Bella's diversion."

Bella snickered. "Nah, they don't know it was me."

"What did you do?" Dad asked her.

"Magic." It was childish to resort to telling tales, I knew, but Bella seemed determined for the world to know about her newfound magical talents. "Of a sort."

"Oh, one of her little trinkets," said Mum. "I'm glad she

found a use for them. She's been causing havoc for months testing them on your father and me."

So they know? Of course. Now that I thought about it, it made perfect sense for my parents to have consented to let Bella make magical bracelets that could set off alarms and throw sparks at people. Their hats could be just as dangerous, after all.

When Bella smirked at me, I rolled my eyes back. "I hope you aren't letting her test them on members of the public. What—?"

Charlie interrupted by launching himself at Sunbeam again. I leapt at him and grabbed for the cat's tail, missing by inches.

"Mum, I told you to keep your familiar under control!" I hadn't meant to yell, but all my frustration came bubbling to the surface. "If we ever find Spencer, I don't want to tell him that your cat *ate* his assistant."

"Charlie!" Mum reprimanded. "Come here and stop that at once."

The cat gave me a begrudging look and slunk over to her side while Sunbeam hid himself behind the tree. Mum and Dad exchanged concerned looks.

"Are you sure we can't help?" asked Dad. "We can pay Janice a visit…"

"Not after Bella threatened her with her magic."

Bella frowned. "You have magic, too, remember?"

"I do, but I don't use it to set off false alarms or kidnap guests from our rival's inn."

"Who said anything about kidnapping?"

"If we hadn't cornered Patricia, that would have been your next idea, wouldn't it?"

"Hey, capturing Janice might convince her to confess…

ELLE ADAMS

joking, joking." Bella ducked as if she thought I might hit
her. "Does she have any friends we can question, then?"

"Not that I move in the same circles as her, so no," I
replied. "And she certainly won't talk to Mercy or me. I'd
say the fact that she purposefully moved her event up so
everyone will get to see her play a day before ours is
enough reason for her to act guilty. It doesn't mean she
kidnapped Spencer."

"You told me she got mad at you yesterday."

"For delivering her mail." I shook my head. "It's been
ages since we had a real argument, and she seems to have
come up with a whole conspiracy on her own."

"Unless she has a genuine reason to believe you'd be
mad at her," added Bella. "There's got to be a way to make
her slip up. Maybe I'll buy a ticket to her event."

I groaned. "If you do, keep me out of it. We have our
own event to plan. If it even goes ahead."

"What do you mean?" asked Mum.

"The choir has flu, and so does most of the theatre
group, including Mercy's boyfriend."

"Oh, no," said Dad. "Want us to come up with a
replacement act?"

"Definitely not. You already have hats to sell, right?"

"We'll do that, then," said Mum. "Really, we want to
help you."

"I know." My voice cracked. "All I wanted was for you
to meet Spencer and for the meeting to go ahead without
a hitch. I knew it wouldn't be simple, but I didn't think
he'd *disappear*. The universe surprised me with that one.
Can I wish for a do-over?"

Bella cleared her throat. "Yes, you can. But you don't
need my advice, clearly."

144

Her words brought me up short. With the wishing box, I *could* wish for a do-over, but the side effects wouldn't be worth it. Then again, was it any worse than waiting until whenever the Fairy Godmother came to town to beg for her help?

I blew out a breath. "I'll wait for Mercy to finish talking to the Fairy Godmother, and we'll see what she says. Can you stay out of trouble until then?"

"If you're sure." Mum beckoned Charlie to follow her to the stairs. "We'll prepare our hats to deliver to our customers."

Dad joined her, while Bella remained behind. As I'd expected. When my parents had vanished upstairs, I went into the back room. Mercy must have gone through the other door into the hall to speak on the phone in privacy, leaving me an opportunity.

I faced the cupboard containing the wishing box, untouched for months. Before I could second-guess myself, I dug out the key and unlocked the cupboard, revealing the sparkling box. I couldn't believe I was even thinking of using it so close to the event, but perhaps I'd made a mistake in leaving everything to chance to begin with.

Bella nudged the door open behind me. "You aren't going to use that, are you?"

"We're going to use it at our event." With restrictions. Presents only. "Seems daft, considering at this rate, nobody will get the gifts they ordered in time for the holidays. Unless they wish for new ones."

"I'm not going to stop you from giving it a test run first," she said. "In fact, that might be a good idea. Have you even touched it since last year?"

"No." I left the box and went looking for my notepad and pen. "Any wish I make has to be free from any loopholes. If I write, *I wish Spencer would come back this afternoon,* does that sound like it would work?"

"Yes, it does." She watched me write it down. "Go on, before you change your mind."

Hardly able to believe I was actually doing this, I fetched the wishing box from the cupboard and brought it to the front desk. Under Bella's watchful eye, I put the piece of paper into the box and closed it.

Then I waited, counting to ten under my breath. When I'd finished, I picked up my phone to call Spencer. If his phone battery was still out, this might not work, but how else would I tell he was back in town?

My call went to voicemail. Again.

"The spell might not have made his phone battery life come back on," Bella said. "If that's the issue."

"No, but I would have thought he'd come straight here as soon as he returned from... wherever he went."

I ran to the door and outside the inn, looking up and down the path. Behind me, Bella walked out with the glittering box in her hands. "Does this thing have an off-on switch?"

"No." I took it from her, and the box's lid came off. The piece of paper lay where I'd put it... but it should have disappeared.

"That's not supposed to happen, is it?" asked Bella.

"No." I backed into the reception area, clutching the box in both hands. "It doesn't last forever. The box, I mean. I don't know how long... Mercy is the one who ordered it, not me."

"You've had it a year, right?"

"We haven't even used it since last year." But it couldn't be clearer that the wish hadn't worked. "Oh, no. *No.*"

Not only had I failed to get Spencer back, but if the wishing box was no longer working, we wouldn't be able to use it in our event, either. Now we were in real trouble.

14

I had to wait for Mercy to finish talking to the Fairy Godmother before I told her the bad news—which also meant admitting I'd tried to use the box without asking her first. Dread coiled within me as I waited, pacing behind the desk. Even Bella had left to give us some privacy to talk over this latest disaster.

Finally, Mercy ducked back into the reception area and went utterly still when she saw me holding the wishing box. "What… are you doing with that?"

"It's broken." My voice cracked. "I'm sorry. I stupidly tried to use it to get Spencer back, and it didn't work. I think we should have checked to make sure it wasn't wearing out before promising to use it in this year's event."

"But… we didn't even use it that much." Her face flushed. "I'm sorry. This is my fault. I'm the one who ordered it."

"A year ago," I reminded her. "I don't blame you for not knowing. Anyway, what did the Fairy Godmother say?"

Mercy's expression brightened a little. "She'll be here tomorrow morning, and she told me she's willing to help us."

"I don't see her agreeing to play Fairy Godmother for everyone at our event, though." Besides, I wouldn't put the burden of fixing everything on her. "What are we supposed to do instead?"

"I'll see if I can get it working." She took the wishing box from me and began scribbling on scraps of paper.

I left her to it, pacing the reception area and trying to think of a way out of this which *didn't* involve making limitless wishes. With the current state of the post office, we had zero chance of ordering a replacement—and we now knew that nobody else in town had one either.

Bella came back downstairs, making so little noise that I had to wonder if she'd been lurking out of sight and eavesdropping on us the whole time.

"You advertised the box as part of the event?" she asked. "There's no way to undo that?"

"No, but absolutely nobody is paying any attention to our event now," I said. "They're too busy looking for their missing mail."

"Or signing up to buy hats," she added.

"That or planning to go to Janice's event instead." I exhaled in a sigh. "All we have now is a bare-bones play with half the cast missing. No wishing box, no carollers… just an excessive number of hats."

"They love our parents' hats, though," said Bella. "You can't deny that."

"I guess not."

This was supposed to be *our* event, though, and while it might be ridiculous to resent my parents for taking over, I could tell from Mercy's distraught expression that she'd had the same thought. The purpose of the event was to draw new eyes onto the inn, but if everyone expected me to start making hats instead, I might as well have stayed at home and worked for my family's business rather than coming here to start one of my own.

I shoved that thought firmly aside. Mercy and I had established our business over the past few years on our own, and nothing would change that. Not Janice's interference, nor anything else. So we didn't have a wishing box. That didn't mean we couldn't think of an alternative, especially with the Fairy Godmother willing to help.

Would three wishes be enough to solve all of this? Or six, if Mercy and I both asked for three? I didn't know.

Mercy put down the wishing box, her hands trembling. "It's defunct. You're right."

"Then we'll take it out of the equation," I said. "We can still ask the Fairy Godmother for help, right?"

"Yeah." She gave a shaky breath. "I don't know… can a wish miraculously cure the flu overnight?"

"It might," I said. "I'd say our priority ought to be stopping the spell affecting everyone's mail."

"Aside from rescuing your missing boyfriend," added Bella.

"I wish I knew where he even *was*." I looked up at the sound of footsteps on the stairs, thinking of Gerry. He had some understanding of that kind of magic, I was sure, but I hadn't been able to make heads or tails of his explanation. If Spencer's disappearance hadn't been caused by a wish after all, then I'd be wasting one of only three wishes on bringing him back when it wouldn't work. Yet as long as I didn't know where he was, I couldn't think of an alternative.

"Maybe he counts as a gift," Bella remarked. "If you wished for him to return as part of fixing the mail service, it might work."

"I didn't order him in the mail, Bella."

Mercy gave a weak chuckle. "You could try it. It can't hurt to combine two wishes into one."

"I'm not so sure." I shook my head. "Don't you want to use one of your wishes for a swift recovery for *your* boyfriend?"

"I'll see what the Fairy Godmother says," she said. "Stopping the packages going missing is our priority, but I'm not sure she can conjure up an alternative to the wishing box for us to use in the event."

Bella lifted her head. "Why can't you wish for a wishing box?"

"I asked her out of curiosity," Mercy said, her face flushing. "She told me her powers avoid loopholes like that."

"Figures." I reached for my notepad again and passed it to Mercy. "You come up with a list of possible wishes. I'll see how Mum and Dad are getting on."

In truth, it was Gerry I wanted to talk to, but I didn't know how to ask him to explain the physics of magically disappearing someone in terms a regular person could understand. All I wanted was to know if it was possible to bring someone back who'd been disappeared, or if it was more probable that he'd been transported to an actual place instead of nowhere.

Up on the second floor, I rapped on the door to the

only occupied room. Gerry appeared in the doorway, clutching a dozen spoons in his hand. "I found them!"

"Oh," I said. "Erm… whereabouts were they?"

"Here and there." He gave a vague gesture at the room, which he seemed to have decorated to resemble a stage. *Hmm.* "It's all about looking in the right place."

"Can you make a person who's been magically vanished show up again?" Did it really matter if he knew the full details? I had to know the truth. "I think someone used a wish to make my boyfriend disappear, and I wanted to know if it's possible to use another one to bring him back."

"With a *wish?*" he echoed. "No, no, you can't wish a person out of existence."

"You can't?" I stared at him. "You mean it isn't possible? He can't have disappeared?"

Then where is he?

His face fell at my expression. "I thought that was good news."

"It is, but I don't know where he is." I backed up a step. "Never mind. Sorry I bothered you."

"It's no problem at all." He held out the handful of spoons. "Want to watch my act?"

"Sure, why not."

The spoons vanished from one of his hands and reappeared in the other. "See? I've finally mastered it."

"You have?" An idea occurred to me. "Ah—would you be willing to help out at our event this Saturday? Half the carollers have come down with flu, and so have a few crucial members of the theatre group. I think a magic show would be a hit."

He beamed. "Yes, I would be delighted to!"

Huh. Maybe he'd come here hoping to perform for us after all and had simply got distracted along the way. Anyone's guess. Maybe Janice had the right idea in inviting her performers to stay at the inn. It would also explain how she'd pulled it together so quickly and without anyone catching the flu.

"You're a lifesaver," I said. "I'll tell Mercy, and we'll work out the details. Then I'll let you know. That okay?"

"Of course!" He withdrew into his room, humming to himself.

I descended the stairs, and Mum and Dad ambushed me on the first floor.

"Everything all right?" Mum asked. "Want to come and help us with the orders?"

"No, thanks." I softened my tone at her crestfallen expression. "I have to help Mercy. The wishing box broke, so we can't use it in the event, but Gerry has a magic act to put on instead. We'll figure it out, but we're going to be rushed off our feet all day."

"Let us know if we can help," Dad said.

"I will do."

I descended the rest of the way to the ground floor and found Mercy wiping her eyes on a tissue. She'd taken the situation even worse than I had, as if she thought it was her own fault for not taking note of the lifespan of the wishing box. It wasn't, not at all, but I understood how defeated she must be feeling.

"Is it okay if we have Gerry put on a magic show on Saturday?" I asked her. "To take some pressure off the theatre group and distract everyone from the missing wishing box?"

"Does he want to?" she asked.

"Yeah, and he seems to have got an act together," I said. "He made all the spoons he lost reappear again—and more importantly, he told me that Spencer can't have vanished because of a wish."

She blinked. "Really?"

"Apparently so."

As for whereabouts he was, though? That remained a mystery that only the Fairy Godmother might be able to help me solve.

———

Mercy and I spent all night redoing our schedule for the event and making a fresh batch of leaflets. I wanted to add *Come to our inn to find your missing packages* to the event list, but that would have to wait until the Fairy Godmother arrived and we could work out if her powers would be able to bring a halt to the spell. Her arrival couldn't come soon enough.

When I got downstairs at dawn after snatching a couple of hours' sleep, I found yet more packages that weren't ours on the doorstep. "Here we go again."

Sunbeam flew out of the inn and tried to pick up one of the smaller packages, but I beckoned him back inside.

"Leave it to the other owls," I told him. "I'll have more leaflets for you to give out later."

Remaking our leaflets had taken half the night, but at least some of the attendees wouldn't come to the inn expecting to be able to make a wish and receive nothing but a hat instead. The wishing box itself had gone missing at some point during the night, but I expected it to show up in Charlie's treasure hoard soon enough. He'd finally stopped trying to catch Sunbeam in favour of playing with the glittering box, apparently finding it more entertaining than chasing the owl. Or perhaps it was because he'd realised that Sunbeam came equipped with pointy claws and wasn't just a fluffy toy. In any case, I was glad that they'd stopped fighting, because today was officially our last chance to launch a successful event.

Mercy came downstairs, not having slept either, and she watched me approach with bloodshot eyes. "More packages?"

"Yep," I said. "Have you heard from the Fairy Godmother yet?"

"No." She yawned. "It's early, though. Your mum and dad aren't going to start selling their hats until what, noon?"

"Yeah," I replied. "Janice's event starts this afternoon, but I think tomorrow's show is going to be different enough that people will go to both."

"Especially if we get their mail back." She jumped when the phone rang and then grabbed it. "Hello—yes, we're here! Come on in!"

A flash of glittering light came from the other side of the front door, near the packages, and a familiar winged shape appeared. My heart lifted. The Fairy Godmother was here.

I hurried outside and circled the pile of boxes to meet her. "You have no idea how glad I am to see you."

"I think I can imagine," she replied. "Has she told you yet?"

"Has who told me what?" I frowned. "Your niece, you mean? She's at Janice's, who's been telling her all sorts of weird lies about how I planned to blackmail her into delivering wishes to you."

"Is that so? I'll put her right on that one."

"Not yet," I said hastily. "You might have gathered we have a mess to clean up here first."

She eyed the stack of packages. "Yes, I imagine you do."

Upon entering the inn after me, she made eye contact with Mercy, who was behind the counter.

"Hey." Mercy had gone bright red for some reason. "I'm glad you're here early."

The Fairy Godmother pursed her lips. "So you didn't tell her."

"Tell me what?" I turned to Mercy. "You're still going to make three wishes, right?"

"No… it's not that." Mercy lowered her gaze, her face as red as Santa's hat. "I… I'm sorry, Carol. I was going to tell you, but not until after I fixed it."

"Fixed what?"

She spoke to the desk. "I'm the one who messed up all the packages, and I don't know how to make it stop."

"You did what?" I stared at her, baffled. "You… did you use the wishing box? Is that why it's not working?"

A tear ran down her cheek. "I was stressed out over the event, and nothing seemed to be going right. When I found out the theatre company's deliveries weren't likely to show up on time, I panicked. There was a delay—a huge one, so I wished our packages would show up on time and somehow screwed up the entire postal system."

"How?" Given the wishing box's track record, perhaps it'd rearranged events so that the theatre company's packages would show up first and accidentally caused some magical aftereffects. "How can the box have done that?"

"I don't know, but I swear I didn't realise until yesterday," she mumbled. "Not until you mentioned the trouble being caused by a wishing box. I thought someone in the post office itself had done it, same as you."

"Then… where's Spencer?"

"I don't know," she whispered, sounding miserable. "I only made the one wish. I don't understand how that could have led to him disappearing."

"It might not have." But something or someone had sent him out of town, and I had no idea where he'd gone. "Janice was right?"

She cringed. "She knew? I thought she might figure it out."

"I don't understand." I was sleep deprived, admittedly, but I'd never thought *Mercy* would have used the wishing box before I did. "However it happened, though, we can fix it with three wishes. Or six."

"No," said Mercy. "Three, not six. I think I've already proven I can't be trusted with wishes."

"You couldn't have known," I protested. "Besides, I can't use one of our important wishes to get Spencer back when a lot of people's holidays are about to be severely disrupted if they don't get their parcels back."

"It's no more selfish than me using the wishing box to fix our event and accidentally screwing up everything else. Less so, if anything."

"Look, one of us was bound to make that mistake eventually," I said. "Also, if it's any consolation, if the wishing box was really that close to drying up, it'd have died in the middle of the event if you hadn't used it to make that wish."

"Oh." She blinked. "You have a point there."

"Exactly," said the Fairy Godmother. "It's up to you what wishes you make, Carol."

"I…" I faltered. I wanted Spencer back, but what if there was a chance that he hadn't disappeared due to a magical accident at all? If he hadn't, then I'd have wasted a wish when I hadn't needed to.

"You don't have to decide just yet," said the Fairy Godmother. "Take your time."

"We're running *out* of time," I said. "Janice's event is taking place today, so if I wish for the gifts to return to their owners, they might not even be home to receive them."

"Best not to," said the Fairy Godmother. "Wishing for every gift to return to a different house has potential for error too. No, your best bet is to wish for them all to appear in one location. Like, say, here."

"Won't they disappear at midnight if nobody claims them?"

"It'll have to be tomorrow, then," said Mercy, some of the misery fading from her expression. "Everyone will already be here to watch the event, and we can use that wish in place of giving everyone access to the wishing box."

"Exactly," I said. "I'll make that wish tomorrow. And the other two…"

For my second wish, I'd ask for a quick recovery for everyone with flu. As for the third…

Footsteps came from the stairs. Then Mum and Dad descended into the reception area, with Bella behind them.

"Ah—this is the Fairy Godmother," I told them. "This is my mum and dad. You've met Bella already."

"I'm Betty, usually, when I'm not 'Fairy Godmother,'" said the Fairy Godmother mildly. "I'm also not staying in town for long… unless you have room at the inn."

"I do." I frowned. "Why did your niece pick Janice's inn instead?"

"I have no idea," she replied. "I'll talk to her and find out. Do you have any rooms available?"

"I—yes, we do. Is the Tooth Fairy coming as well?" The two had been an item since summer, so I was surprised he hadn't come with her.

"If that's okay with you." She smiled. "Sorry for the short notice. The truth is, we intended to surprise you at your event, but when Mercy called me, I knew you needed me early. But yes, I've been planning to come back here for a while, and I've always been interested to meet your family."

"Don't tell me you want to buy a hat."

She merely grinned, but I couldn't fault her for being drawn to my parents' hats when she might just have saved the show. We did have a spare room opposite Gerry's too.

"Think about the other wishes," said the Fairy Godmother. "I'm going to speak to Patricia."

"Watch out for Janice," I warned. "I thought she was being irrational, but maybe she did guess that our wishing box caused her mail to disappear. Oh, and she *might* have caused Spencer to disappear herself after he left her inn. No idea how, though."

"I'll have a look around," said the Fairy Godmother. "Don't worry about me. I don't scare easily."

"Janice won't know what hit her." Bella smirked. "As for Spencer, I have an idea."

"It doesn't involve one of those spells of yours, does it?" I asked warily.

"Nope, believe it or not," she said. "I think you should tell the post office staff about the Fairy Godmother's plan to return the mail to its owners tomorrow."

"You mean warn them?" Not a terrible idea, though it wouldn't help me find Spencer... or maybe it would, if Travis *had* been behind that particular prank.

"I agree," said the Fairy Godmother. "Tell them about the plan. I'll meet you back here in an hour."

It was time to speak to the staff at the post office again... and this time I wasn't leaving until I had some answers.

15

This time I went to the post office alone, with Sunbeam perched on my shoulder. When I entered, he let out a full-volume hoot that instantly drew all eyes towards us. I probably looked a sight, sleepless and with my hair a mess, but I didn't care. I had the solution to all their problems, and even Dennis wouldn't be able to argue otherwise.

I hoped not, at any rate.

Sure enough, Dennis emerged from his office to see what the noise was. "I have had it with that owl. And *what* are you doing here?"

"I know how to stop the spell messing with the deliveries," I told everyone in the post room. "I thought you'd want to know you don't have to overextend yourselves any longer. All your problems will be solved tomorrow."

"You!" said the elf. "What nonsense is this?"

I addressed him directly. "It might interest you to know that I have a guest at my inn who can stop the packages from vanishing *and* save Christmas for everyone. If you want to tell the owl postmasters in person, I'm sure they'll be glad to hear the news."

Questions arose from the others, but Dennis cut through them all. "I will have nothing to do with that wishing box!"

He knew we had it? I knew better than to tell *him* the real cause of the missing packages, but that didn't mean I couldn't address his concerns.

"The wishing box has broken," I said. "The solution I'm talking about is the Fairy Godmother, who's happy to help us out—but I'll only accept her help with conditions."

"What?" Dennis stared at me. "Do you think you can bargain with me? Really?"

"I need the answer to a simple question," I went on. "Whoever tells me where Spencer is will be single-handedly responsible for saving Christmas."

That was a stretch—I'd freely admit it—but if a wish hadn't been involved in Spencer's disappearance, the post office was where he'd last been seen.

"I told you, I don't know where he is," snarled Dennis. "If I had to guess, he got tired of all the deliveries and left town."

"My other condition is that you don't punish Sunbeam for anything he did while looking for Spencer." I might as well push my advantage while Travis worked up the nerve to admit to what he'd done. I'd given him the chance to confess to me already, so it wasn't my fault he'd have to do so in front of an audience. "Including the incident yesterday."

"I knew that was your doing." Dennis scowled. "If I say yes, then your Fairy Godmother can truly wave her magic wand and fix all of this, can she?"

"Once we know where Spencer is, yes." I watched Travis pointedly. "I have reason to believe the last person who saw him was employed here at this very office."

"I don't know where he is!" Travis burst out in a panic, his gaze darting around. "I really don't."

"But you have an idea, don't you?" I approached him. "What did you do?"

Everyone turned towards him, including the boss, and his shoulders slumped. "He was in one of our sleighs the last time I saw him, looking for extra packages to deliver."

"And?"

"And... erm." He faltered. "I may have shoved him into an empty box and let the sleigh carry him off, so he might have gone anywhere."

"You did *what?*" I swivelled to face Dennis. "Whereabouts do your delivery sleighs end up, the North Pole?"

"Eventually," he growled. "That's no excuse for him not calling the office, though."

"His phone battery was running out the last I heard from him," I informed him. "With everything going on, he hadn't had time to go home and charge it. Anyway, I bet it's a nightmare to find a way back from the North Pole this close to Christmas, when everyone is trying to get home for the holidays."

If he was still stranded there, then I'd need transport of my own to get him back. Which I didn't have... but the post office certainly did.

"Travis," Dennis growled. "You are to drive Miss... Carol, is it? Drive her to the North Pole and pick up our missing employee."

"What?" He wanted me to travel in a sleigh with Travis

of all people? He made a spluttering noise, looking just as outraged as me.

"You heard me," said Dennis. "That's my only offer. Take it or leave it."

"If I don't come back, then the deal is off." As he began to argue, I cut him off. "The Fairy Godmother is answering to me alone. It's not a condition; it's a fact."

Dennis's glare fixated on Travis. "Then you'd better do your job."

The elf wasn't budging, and I could sort of see why he'd choose to send away his laziest employee on this errand. Besides, to get Spencer back, I was willing to put up with anything, even a ride with Travis. Maybe I'd have a nap on the way.

"All right," I said. "As soon as me *and* Spencer are back, I'll tell the Fairy Godmother what to do. Only then."

Travis flushed. "I won't leave you stranded, I swear."

"Good enough." I faced the boss again. "Oh, and once this is solved, I'd appreciate it if you give all your employees Christmas Day off. *And* the Yule Ball."

"That's enough conditions!" When everyone in the office gave him expectant looks, however, his shoulders slumped a little. "Fine. *Only* if everything is delivered as planned. Now, go away."

———

Travis, to my surprise, was on his best behaviour. The threat of retaliation from his boss had apparently convinced him not to leave me in a snowdrift, though the fact that only I could solve the problem of the never-ending deliveries might have had an impact too. In any case, he didn't speak to me as he drove the sleigh, while I caught up on sleep during the long drive up to the North Pole.

Several hours later, I woke up when Sunbeam poked me in the leg. The owl had come with me, of course, eager to find Spencer and bring him back to Holiday Haven.

"We're here," Travis muttered without looking at me. "Go and find him. If you take more than an hour, I'll drive back without you."

I hopped out of the sleigh into the snow, Sunbeam taking flight overhead. He'd obviously had a nap, too, and he'd also exercised a considerable level of restraint in not pecking Travis nonstop throughout our journey.

"Let's find Spencer," I said to him.

Sunbeam hooted and then flew away down the snowy street, while I waited for him to return. Several other sleighs were parked nearby, while humans and elves and other delivery people carried packages around. Considering the number of people around, I was starting to wonder if I'd need to hold up a sign with Spencer's name on it in order to find him. Several minutes had passed before Sunbeam's loud hooting drifted over the sleighs.

I hurried in the direction of the noise and spied Spencer near a red-clad group of elves. He looked tired and dishevelled, but I was so glad to see him at all that I didn't care. Hands shaking with relief, I flung myself at him and hugged him.

"I'm so glad you're here," he said. "I don't have any money with me, and nobody would let me hitch a ride on a sleigh to get back to Holiday Haven. How'd you know I was here?"

"Travis," I answered. "He's the reason you ended up stuck, which I'm guessing you knew."

He rubbed the back of his neck. "I have a few words to say to him. I don't know if he intended to let me out of the box eventually, but I'd hardly been in there five minutes before the sleigh started moving. Next thing I knew, I was on my way to the North Pole."

"It took me a while to get Travis to confess, but I knew it was him," I said. "And you'll have your chance to talk to him. Dennis made him bring me to find you."

"Bet he loved that," he commented. "That means he's driving us back?"

"Unless you want to leave *him* stranded." I grinned. "I'm tempted. I've been going mad trying to find out who took you."

"You didn't think it was the same wish that screwed up the mail, did you?" he asked. "Because it's even happening here too."

My heart dropped. "No... but I did find out the cause and how to stop it. I'll tell you everything on the way back."

"All right." He walked with me to the sleigh, where his eyes narrowed at Travis. "Thought you were being funny, did you?"

Travis went brick red. "You aren't going to leave me behind?"

"I think Dennis the Menace's punishment will make you wish I had." He climbed into the sleigh, as did I, while Sunbeam settled happily between us. "Ride on."

Travis muttered something uncomplimentary under his breath but obeyed him.

"How'd you convince the boss to help you find me?"

Spencer asked in an undertone. "I didn't think he liked me that much."

"The Fairy Godmother is here," I told him. "She's going to fix the situation with the spell…and I made your safe return a condition of helping him out."

I told him everything on the long ride back to Holiday Haven, keeping my voice down so Travis wouldn't overhear us. Eventually I dozed off in Spencer's arms, and we both woke up when the sleigh pulled up in front of the inn.

"Get out," Travis said sourly. "Go on."

"Thanks for the lift," I said breezily. "Say hi to Dennis for me."

Spencer chuckled under his breath and hopped out of the sleigh, holding out a hand to help me climb after him. The inn's doors opened, and the Fairy Godmother emerged, beaming at me. "There you are."

"Guess you're back from speaking to Patricia." I indicated Spencer. "You've met before."

"We have." Spencer smiled at her. "Hey, Betty. And… oh, hey, Carol's parents."

"You must be Spencer!" Mum and Dad both tried to hug him at once, which he tolerated with patience. This wasn't the meeting any of us had imagined, of course, but it was a miracle worthy of a wish that I'd got to introduce him to my parents at all. And we hadn't even needed to use a wish in the process.

"We'll have to meet properly later," Spencer told my family. "I should head back to the post office before Dennis sends out a search party."

"I already told him to give you the holidays off," I added. "As a condition."

"He went for that?"

"He really wants this problem fixed." I shot him a grin. "Please tell me what he does to Travis. Assuming he hasn't driven that sleigh into the wilderness, never to be seen again."

He smiled back. "I can't wait to find out."

After a quick hug and kiss goodbye, he left the inn.

"That took longer than I expected," said Mercy from behind the desk. "Where was he?"

"The North Pole, thanks to a certain co-worker of his," I explained. "He got stranded with no working phone at the busiest time of year."

She grimaced. "I'm glad I didn't cause that one at least."

"We're going to fix the rest." With Spencer up to speed on almost every detail of the plan, all we had to do was put it into action.

The Fairy Godmother was ready to make my wishes come true. And this time, I wouldn't let there be any mistakes.

16

Saturday morning dawned, and I awoke feeling well rested for the long day ahead of me. Mercy and I met with the Fairy Godmother in the lobby to discuss our plans, since the main event wouldn't start until the afternoon. Mum and Dad had almost sold out of their entire stock of hats yesterday, but they'd been up all night making new ones to sell during the interval. The hats covered the entire front desk.

"Are you sure you want to make the wish in front of the audience?" asked the Fairy Godmother.

I inclined my head. "That way they'll all be able to see it. There'll be no ambiguity, so nobody will be able to try to take any gifts that aren't theirs."

There was still a risk that not everyone missing a parcel would show up. But as we'd arranged yesterday, the post owls would be on hand waiting to take the leftover parcels to their owners, and Bella and Travis would supervise to make sure nobody swiped a parcel that wasn't theirs. According to Spencer, the latter had been tasked with overseeing the whole thing, as punishment for his antics this week. Served him right.

As for the theatre group? Daryl had indeed made a complete recovery, and they'd gathered for a very last-minute rehearsal at the studio this morning. Mercy gave me the updates while I hurried around the inn, making a few final tweaks.

At noon, we opened our doors. The inn was packed within an hour, a steady stream of arrivals filing into the lobby while Mum and Dad's hats sang carols in the background. Everyone took their seats in the hall, and I joined them.

When the lights went out, I couldn't help feeling a quiver of nerves. We hadn't been able to tell everyone in advance about the change in plans, and some of them might not be expecting it all. Still, the play had everyone entertained, as did my parents' hat sales in the interval. Gerry also brought out his repertoire of magic tricks, and while not all of them worked, his look of vague confusion was amusement enough on its own.

After the second half of the play had come to a close, Mercy and I approached the front of the hall and climbed onto the stage. With a microphone in my hand, I cleared my throat to get the crowd's attention.

"Hey, everyone." I spoke into the microphone, glad of the darkness that hid the number of faces watching me. We'd ended up having to bring in extra chairs. "I'm glad you could make it to the Holiday Haven Inn's celebration. I have a couple of announcements to make, and I think they'll be of interest to all of you."

"Firstly," Mercy said into her own microphone, "I'm afraid the wishing box is no longer working."

A murmur of dismay passed through the crowd.

"The good news is that we have a special guest here to make up for it." I gestured to the side of the stage. "Please welcome the Fairy Godmother."

Dressed in a bright-pink hat and holding up her sparkling wand, the Fairy Godmother appeared in a puff of smoke to a chorus of cheers.

"I hear there's been some trouble with missing packages this week," she said, not needing a microphone to project her voice across the hall. "Luckily, I'm here to fix the situation."

After the cheers died out, I spoke. "I wish that every parcel in Holiday Haven affected by the spell causing them to disappear would appear within this hall right this instant."

With a wave of the Fairy Godmother's wand, packages began to appear in all corners of the hall. Gasps rang out among the crowd, and Bella hurried into view. An alarm rang out from the bracelet on her wrist, halting everyone before they trampled one another.

"Please proceed in an orderly fashion," Mercy ordered. "One row at a time, and no treading on each other. There's plenty of time."

The crowd obeyed, for the most part, while Bella and Travis looked on. As everyone lined up to claim their packages, I recognised a few people among them. The Tooth Fairy sat beaming at the Fairy Godmother from the audience, while I also saw the Easter Bunny and Cupid near the back. The latter wore the hat he'd acquired last summer, which Bella and I had created to stop him from accidentally bewitching people. It must have worked out for him, because he was all but anonymous amid the crowd.

The theatre group joined the line, and Daryl waved to Mercy. I nudged her towards him, while I squeezed past the crowd to my parents. They'd set up the rest of their hats for sale at the reception, though they didn't have many customers at the moment. Except—

When I looked in her direction, Patricia flinched and then recovered herself. "Sorry. I... wow, there's a lot of people here."

"Yeah, your aunt's spell worked perfectly," I said. "She got everyone's mail back."

"Good," she said. "Sorry I suspected you of trying to steal her wishes. I really didn't know."

"It's fine." I hadn't had the chance to talk to her the previous day, though the Fairy Godmother had filled her in on anything important. "Janice is... well, I don't expect an apology, but she did have a reason to suspect."

"That's no excuse for lying to me," she said. "I... I told her to come here and apologise."

"You did?" I glanced around and saw Janice lurking outside the door as if unwilling to come in. "Let's get this over with, then."

I left the inn and approached Janice, whose expression resembled mine whenever my parents' hats started singing in an inappropriate scenario.

"Carol," she said. "What's going on in there?"

"A last-minute schedule change." I kept my tone polite despite the awkwardness in the air around us. "I'm glad your event went well yesterday... I guess you probably want to pick up your mail, right? Any missing packages are in the hall."

"They are?" She blinked. "Oh, right. No, I don't have any more packages to collect… I just wanted to say I'm sorry."

She mumbled the last words, but I decided not to push for a more sincere apology. "Accepted. Merry Christmas."

She turned around and left with an expression of relief on her face, while I glimpsed several post owls perched in the nearby trees. If they were here, then so was…

A flutter of wings came from above, and Sunbeam descended to greet me. I caught him in my hand and spied Spencer approaching the inn.

I ran to meet him, and he wrapped me in a warm hug. "It went well, then?"

"Yeah, so far." I blew out a breath. "They're mostly behaving themselves, though Bella is on hand to grab anyone who tries to take what isn't theirs."

"Good," he said. "The owls will take care of the rest."

"Travis looks thrilled."

"It's his own fault," he said. "Dennis is being a grump, too, but he's never happy."

"Someone has to be the resident Scrooge." From inside the inn, I spied my parents trying to catch my gaze. "I think Mum and Dad want to talk to you."

"To pick up my hat order, I know."

"Spencer." I looked at him in mild horror. "You didn't."

"Joking." He cracked a grin. "They're not *that* bad, you know."

"I know, I know." I squeezed his hand. "Let's go and talk to them."

We entered the inn, while the sound of everyone in the

hall claiming their gifts mingled with the carols from my parents' hats. This holiday would be an occasion to remember.

ABOUT THE AUTHOR

Elle Adams lives in the middle of England, where she spends most of her time reading an ever-growing mountain of books, planning her next adventure, or writing. Elle's books are humorous mysteries with a paranormal twist, packed with magical mayhem.

She also writes urban and contemporary fantasy novels as Emma L. Adams.

Visit http://www.elleadamsauthor.com/ to find out more about Elle's books.

Printed in the USA
CPSIA information can be obtained
at www.ICGtesting.com
LVHW090039030924
789900LV00031B/260

9 798759 493839